THE GHOST OF
CHE GUEVARA

Jason Webb

THE GHOST OF CHE GUEVARA

MACMILLAN NEW WRITING

First published 2006 by Macmillan New Writing,
an imprint of Macmillan Publishers Ltd
Brunel Road, Basingstoke RG21 6XS
Associated companies throughout the world
www.macmillannewwriting.com

ISBN-13: 978–0230–00100–8 hardback
ISBN-10: 0230–00100–9 hardback
ISBN-13: 978–0230–00742–0 paperback
ISBN-10: 0230–00742–2 paperback

9 8 7 6 5 4 3 2 1

A CIP catalogue record for this book is available from
the British Library.

Typeset by Heronwood Press
Printed and bound in China

One

The doctor giggled and asked them to guess his age.

"Thirty-five," said Pacho.

"No, that's not right. And you? How old do you think I am?"

They could hear birdsong and, a short distance away, someone slowly shovelling.

"You're forty-two."

"Ha!" The doctor straightened his back in his canvas folding chair, so it creaked. "I am eleven years older than that."

The olive-green tarpaulin sagged above them and the still air smelt of damp earth. Robert wiped the sweat from his forehead with the palm of his hand. His mouth was dry and his legs itched from mosquito bites.

"That's incredible," said Pacho.

The doctor nodded.

"People always think I am much younger than I really am. Of course black skin doesn't age so quickly."

His shirt was neatly pressed and he wore polished leather shoes despite the mud. He had begun talking to them without asking their names or offering his own and had revealed his profession but not his reason for being in the camp.

1

"Do you think Alfredo's coming soon?" Robert had whispered to Pacho.

"He'll come when he wants to."

It was always like that. You always had to wait.

A round-faced young woman in bulky army fatigues and thigh-length rubber boots placed aluminium mess cans of sweet black coffee on the wooden table before them and smiled before trudging back down the trail into the jungle. With one hand she supported the strap of an assault rifle slung across her back and with the other she held a floral-patterned plastic tray.

The doctor, raising an eyebrow as he plucked a twig from his coffee, proceeded upon the subject of mortality.

"The key is diet. It determines everything, from weight to energy levels to prostate function. For many men of my age, for example, the prostate is beginning to play up. There is a genetic component of course, but too much fat and red meat is a major cause. Fortunately, in my case, I have always looked after myself and eaten lots of vegetables and fruit, and so I don't have to get up to urinate three or four times a night."

"Is that right?" said Pacho.

"You'd be horrified to know how many men suffer from enlargement of the prostate."

So Robert asked, "But it's mainly in older guys, I mean, guys over fifty, isn't it?"

"Well, it's supposed to be," said the doctor. Then he described how, in a nearby town, he had once detected cases of swollen prostate in all of the adult male inhabitants. The most likely cause was the use of the local brothels. The prostate acts as a repository of venereal bacteria, which collect in it and multiply. Robert wanted to know about symptoms, and the doctor seemed to enjoy making his reply.

"After you finish urinating, you should only need to shake yourself two or three times. Any more than that is masturbation," he said, "No, thank you."

Pacho had leant across the table, offering a packet of cigarettes.

"They poke you up your arse, don't they? I mean, when they test you," he said.

Cupping his hands, he flicked at a lighter and then stopped, extracting the cigarette from his mouth still unlit.

"He's here," he said, and the three of them rose to their feet.

They saw the doctor again in the evening, but this time he didn't want conversation. After being fed chicken and rice in the rebel camp, they had gone out to see if they could find a place selling beer, and had walked in the dark down a dirt road to a village that stretched a short way along a single street. They found him sitting in the glow of the food shack where people gathered to watch the only local television set. He was accompanied by one of the rebel commanders, and they both ignored Robert and Pacho as they made their way through the crowd to the uneven wooden bar.

3

It wasn't much of a restaurant: just another timber hut with plastic tables and chairs lain in view of a kitchen where a cook in dirty flip flops prepared rice and beans and thin slices of fried meat. Naked electric light bulbs made the place seem very bright after the darkness outside. It was full of campesinos wearing dirty t-shirts and jeans, sitting at metal tables loaded with beer cans and dusty soft drink bottles, and they looked sideways at the journalist and his cameraman. Some of the peasants smiled shyly, not looking at them. But they weren't friendly smiles; they were nervous, voyeuristic smiles anticipating something unusual or violent, like the smiles some people make after seeing a car crash.

"Look at that," said Pacho, handing Robert the two cold cans of Aguila beer he had just paid for.

A man sitting at a table close to the television set was using an old fashioned set of metal scales to weigh plastic bags of the white coca paste which is used to make cocaine. Before weighing each bag he tested its purity by taking a sample with a spoon and heating it with a cigarette lighter, so it spat and fizzed. At the same time, he was watching the television like everyone else, and the other people in the restaurant didn't pay any attention to him.

Quietly, his eyes still fixed before him, Pacho slipped his hands into his rucksack and took out a small video camera. He removed its cloth cover and managed to film for several seconds before someone whispered a warning. Then the old man stood up in front of the scales, pulled his broad-brimmed hat down over his face and scooped up the small

4

packets of paste before putting his head down and shuffling off through the bar. The other customers pretended not to notice and Pacho turned off the camera and slipped it back into its cover. The shots would make good B-roll.

He smiled at Robert and wiped the rim of his beer with a folded paper napkin before tugging back its tab.

"They don't want no publicity," he said in English and leant against the bar.

Whole skinny families had come to the restaurant to watch the television. Wives sat at tables with their husbands, dandling babies on their knees. Small children, their heads daubed with cheap cologne, ran out to the road and in again, dodging between the adults. One boy stood petting a small, grasping, monkey-like Amazon animal with a snout like a fox's.

The television was showing the evening news. But the reactions of the people in the restaurant were exactly opposite to those intended by the broadcasters. The campesinos laughed with complicity at archive footage showing the Revolutionary Armed Forces of Colombia and shook their heads when an army general claimed a victory. Only when the entertainment section began, with its soft-porn shots of silicone-inflated beauties and gossip about actors, did the village audience relax and become uncritical, anticipating with pleasure the long lullaby hours of soap operas which each night reconciled them to the sleepy walk down the dirt road to the musty darkness of their huts.

Robert said, "The poor bastard. Don't you think he's

5

going to turn out to be a poor, stupid bastard?"

"I don't know. Maybe."

And Pacho laughed quietly, his mouth open.

"But we've got to wait," said Robert, inhaling between gritted teeth, hoping to conjure bad luck. "We've got to wait."

He finished his beer quickly and signalled for two more

"How did it seem to you? How do you think it went?" he asked. He avoided the word "Alfredo".

"It went okay. Not bad. When he wants to do something, he gets it done, and he thinks he can get something out of us, so it probably will get done."

They were watching the TV over the rows of nodding baseball hats and shining black hair.

"Yes, he thinks he can get something out of us," said Robert, and Pacho nodded and smiled.

Pacho was really very ugly. His face, discoloured and loose-skinned on top of a sparse yet pot-bellied body, looked as if it had just begun to melt. Its proportions were distorted, as if he had moved too quickly in a photograph. But somehow this unattractiveness, combined with a certain cool, a certain wary poise, leant him gravitas, a sad seriousness. Robert liked this about Pacho, along with the fact that people occasionally mistook him for a hitman, granting Robert by implication the flattering status of hitman's accomplice.

They had come to do a story about an American who had joined the FARC. At first, when Robert had heard the rumour, he hadn't believed it, but Pacho had spoken to his contact and now Alfredo had given them permission to speak to the man.

Pacho ordered more beer, and they sucked them back quickly. It was hot inside the bar.

"I was hoping to drink less on this trip," said Robert, "I thought I wouldn't be able to get any and I'd be forced to go without alcohol. And that wouldn't have been a bad thing."

"I don't know. I like a beer as well as you do. I think it's good we can get it."

Pacho was at home with his defects. He made them seem interesting.

"Okay. Just one more, and then let's go," said Robert.

Aguila was one of those drinks which wasn't worth having, but which you have anyway, to assuage a drinker's greedy anxiety, the fear that you might be missing out on a good thing. They had a couple of rounds more and then made their way to the door. The other customers tracked them from the corners of their eyes. The doctor and his guerrilla friend were no longer sitting outside. Local people had occupied their seats on the street and were looking into the restaurant, watching the television as if they were in the back row of a cinema.

The night air seemed cool after the crowded bar. They followed the dirt road away from the shacks and into the darkness, picking their way carefully between rocks and potholes. Tall trees fringed the stars with slowly swaying shadows of absolute black. Suddenly, as if he had tuned in on a radio dial, Robert became aware of the whirr and buzz of innumerable insects. And their voices and the crunch of their feet on the road sounded loud in the jungle night.

"Do you think the insects make more of a noise after dark, or is it just that we don't notice them during the day?"

Pacho considered the question gravely, and then replied, "I don't know, but it's an interesting point. Tomorrow I'll listen, if I don't forget."

They almost missed the entrance to the camp in the dark. A sentry allowed them to pass, and another guerrilla shined a torch on the track when Robert stumbled. He bent down to slither into his small tent, which was really just a tarpaulin pegged low over some planks of wood covered with dry palm fronds where he had laid out his kit. Once again, the weirdness of the situation was disorienting. It was as if cotton wool had been packed around the sharp edges of reality, disappointing almost, the way he often didn't feel that what was happening had anything to do with him. The insects hissed and hummed. In the dark, he took off his boots and laid them by his sleeping bag before zipping himself up, still wearing his socks. He would never have thought it, but it could be cold in the jungle at night.

Two young bodyguards had trotted behind Alfredo as he strode through the clearing and up to the bivouac. All carried Kalashnikovs strapped to their backs, but Alfredo also wore a pistol in a holster on his hip, like an officer in a real army.

Waving his hand, Alfredo had told the doctor to go and wait for him elsewhere. Then he had raised his unshaven double chin and turned to Pacho, who transferred his cigarette to his left hand and wiped his right on his trouser leg before holding it out to be shaken.

Alfredo was still speaking to Pacho when he took Robert's hand, looking at him with narrowed eyes. His manner was one of menacing humour, as if he wanted to bully people into enjoying being bullied.

"And so this is the gringo?"

"Yes, *comandante*," said Pacho, "He's called Robert Hoggard."

"Tall, isn't he? The son of a bitch."

Robert stood stooping under the low tarpaulin.

Still gripping his hand, Alfredo smiled and made a joke about kidnapping him. Everything Alfredo said was clearly funny if he meant it to be, so everyone laughed. Pacho laughed, as did Alfredo's bodyguards and of course Robert too, although he tried, impossibly, to do so with dignity.

Alfredo persisted with his joke.

"Would your family miss you?"

"I certainly hope so."

"They would?"

"I hope so," repeated Robert. He made an effort to grin and cleared his throat.

Alfredo let go.

"Son of a bitch. They'd pay up then. What do you want? Whisky? Vodka?"

9

It was barely ten o'clock in the morning, but Pacho thanked him and asked for a whisky. Robert followed his lead, although it occurred to him that perhaps vodka was more revolutionary. Alfredo sent one of his escorts to fetch the drinks and unslung his assault rifle, placing it on the table. His movements were unusually quick, especially for such a portly man, like Henry the Eighth playing tennis, and he sunk into his seat with evident relief, sighing and removing his beret to dry his head with a handkerchief. To Robert's surprise, a long, greasy lock of hair had been wound around a bald dome, and Alfredo slyly rearranged this threadbare natural turban with a twirl of his fingers before replacing his beret and leaning back in his chair, tugging one end of his moustache.

He looked at Pacho, waving his hand in Robert's direction.

"And this gringo, how do I know he's not some CIA agent?"

Robert wasn't sure whether this was another joke, but Pacho answered.

"Alfredo, he is a journalist. We've worked together for a long time."

"Sometimes you can't tell."

"I am a journalist. Of course I am a journalist," said Robert. He cleared his throat again and explained who he worked for, but this only seemed to bore the rebel commander.

"I know that you are a journalist, otherwise you wouldn't be here," he said.

A bottle of Scotch was placed on the table before them, with three small glasses.

"We would have identified you and put you away somewhere safe."

He looked at the bottle and pursed his lips.

"I will just taste. I can't drink it. They won't let me, for my health."

They clinked glasses. Alfredo took a sip of his whisky, swilled it in his mouth, and spat it on the ground.

"Damn," he said, looking at the small puddle of alcohol. Then he slapped his hands on the table. Robert noticed they had been manicured, his nails clipped and polished.

"To business, boys," he said, and the phrase sounded incongruous. "What is it that you need? I'm in a hurry."

Alfredo wanted to be assured their interests coincided, and perhaps they did. While his tone was authoritative, he had a thick peasant accent and spoke quickly, so Robert, whose Spanish was only passable, had difficulty understanding much of what he said. But Pacho, finally taking advantage of a chance to light his cigarette, acted as his representative during the initial banter. He flattered the commander and told him that if they did a story about his American fighter it would illustrate the idealism of the FARC and the way the rebels sacrificed themselves to fight for the poor.

One of the bodyguards, slouching against a tree, was wearing a black t-shirt printed with the handsome but slightly neanderthal face of Che Guevara. Many of the guerrillas wore t-shirts like that. The world was one big, self-referential mess of pop culture, although the rebels still killed people of course, and got killed themselves: that was still completely real.

"I want you to show the human side of my guerrillas," said Alfredo, enthusiastic now, and Robert marvelled at the facility of cliché to penetrate even the Colombian jungle.

Alfredo extemporised, the rhythm of his speech marked by a plosive snare drum of obscenity. "A guerrilla has discipline, dedication, *hijueputa*. I want people to see they aren't the son-of-a-bitch murderers those *hijueputa* oligarchs say they are."

"That's what we want to do, *comandante*," said Pacho, "Oh yes, that's exactly what we want to do."

Two

Passing through a coca-growing town a few days earlier they had seen the corpse of a farmer in a white plastic chair on a concrete porch in the sun. The force of the bullets that killed him had tilted the chair back against a brick wall, lifting the man's feet off the ground, and his head had slumped against his right arm, which was supported by the rim of the chair and extended stiffly above a jelly of blood and brains. He had been a heavy man, and the bulge of his paunch under a sweaty blue t-shirt made Robert think of a dead dog swelling in the heat. A police officer was going through his pockets and laid his possessions – a rubber Disney key ring, some coins, a wallet stuffed with cash – on a sheet of black plastic. A crowd of local people had gathered to gape, and spoke to each other in whispers. They didn't seem surprised or shocked. A small boy giggled, and some of the adults were smirking, as if they had made a clever point merely by staying alive. Only one person wept – a teenage girl in flip-flops who stared at her blue-painted toenails, one hand pushed into her mouth.

"How about it?"

They were standing behind the crowd, on a dirt road.

"It's a good image. You don't get these very often," said

Pacho, with a shrug, waiting for Robert to decide something. "I've got the small camera," he said.

So Pacho began to film and Robert identified himself to a police lieutenant who was counting bullet holes in the wall. He didn't want to speak but couldn't refuse.

"The people never see anything here. They clam up. It's useless," said the lieutenant, as his men stared at Pacho. Robert noticed a military guard post just twenty or thirty metres down the road, two soldiers looking small with their guns behind waist-high sandbags.

"Paramilitaries?" insisted Robert, frowning professionally, feeling the sun burning the crown of his head.

"If only people would talk."

A police pick-up truck nudged through the crowd, and a public prosecutor, avoiding Robert, beckoned to the lieutenant. Officers began to bend the dead man's hairy limbs to zip him into a body bag, and a woman was waiting with a bucket to wash away the mess.

Pacho put away the camera. "Let's go," he said, and they walked away between the low houses, not looking back.

"They didn't like that very much," said Robert.

They returned to their hotel, where they had already left their bags. It had no hot water but the rooms were air-conditioned and there was cable television, which, in addition to the usual signal, also showed channels from Peru and Bolivia. They waited until dusk, and then went out again, taking an intentionally winding route through the powdery back streets.

The contact they had come to meet was a stocky middle-aged woman who had just washed her long hair with water from a barrel and was wringing it dry. She brought them fresh lemonade as they sat sweating in her metal-roofed parlour, where a tiny dog chewed raw meat on the bare concrete before them.

"We saw a guy who'd just been killed," said Pacho.

She shook her head, with its heavy, wet, grey hair. She had heard about it. It was obvious who had killed him, but this was one of those towns where it was better to mind your own business.

Robert let Pacho do most of the talking. He hadn't thought she was a member of the FARC, but she knew how to find them all right. When they had finished, they escorted her to a service in a brightly-lit evangelical church installed in a large shed, and she had said goodbye with a happy smile like a girl's.

They had almost made it back to their hotel when they were stopped by a couple of teenage soldiers. They had walked right past them and Robert could see them making up their minds to stop them. But they had already passed them when one of the soldiers put his fingers in his mouth and whistled.

"Hey, you two. Up against the wall."

Robert placed his hands against a wall beneath a street-lamp. One of the soldiers frisked him and then he stood up straight again.

"Papers. What's your business here?"

But Robert had gone mute. He couldn't answer questions. He didn't know if it was from fear or anger. He looked down at the soldier pointing a gun at him. The guy was about eighteen years old. He was a runt. The soldier bared his teeth as he gripped his gun and he couldn't stop his voice from trembling. He hunched his scrawny shoulders and lowered his head like a skinny bull that wanted to butt.

Pacho spoke for Robert.

"He's English," he said, "He's been registered with the authorities."

The second soldier was more relaxed, and perhaps more cautious.

"English from England, or English from the United States?" he asked, and they let them go quite soon.

Back in the hotel, in Robert's room, Pacho sat down on the shabby bed and lit a cigarette.

"That guy was afraid of us," said Robert.

"Dangerous."

"With us they wouldn't dare."

"They're scared of what we filmed."

Robert took two beers out of the rusty minibar.

"They're not going to touch us."

Pacho exhaled.

"No, of course not."

"They wouldn't dare. It would cause them problems."

"Of course, it would cause them problems."

Pacho paused and then he said, "Now if we had been locals, some unimportant little shits from around here, and the soldiers were worried, they'd take us back to the barracks. And then ..."

He passed a finger across his throat.

"Shit," said Robert.

He always hoped that if he voiced a fear then Pacho would reassure him, and he would be able to draw comfort because Pacho was Colombian and experienced. But it never seemed to work like that.

Pacho continued, "It has happened many times. Every day it happens."

"What a lovely town."

"What I'm worried about is that they could call their friends. That would be easy."

"Shit."

"It wouldn't be logical, but they're worried, so they make one telephone call and it's too late. And those paramilitaries, if they kill you, they do it with malice, so you know about it. I hate that."

Robert sat down on the bed. Pacho got up.

"I'm going to go and watch the news," he said.

"We've still got to eat."

"After the news."

"We should stay in the hotel, don't you think?"

"It would be best."

Robert had left his tape recorder and notebook on the bed, and, once alone, he shifted them unnecessarily. He inspected the door which led onto a narrow second-floor balcony. Then he switched on the air conditioner embedded in the wall beneath cheap beige curtains, and it shuddered and droned, blowing out dust. He turned on the television. The pretty female newsreader was recounting the day's murder and mayhem, but he couldn't pay attention, so he had another beer.

As he drank, he found increasing consolation in the thought that Pacho was also very jumpy. After a third beer he felt considerably better and went and knocked on Pacho's door. He had been drinking more beer too.

"We should go and get something to eat," said Robert.

The idea just seemed more obvious now.

"Yeah."

"But is there anything in the hotel?"

"No. Not in the hotel."

"But we've got to eat."

"We've got to eat."

"We'll be careful."

"Yeah. Let's be quick."

"Close to the hotel, eh," said Robert. "We don't want to walk around so much drawing attention to ourselves."

The stars, like weak lights in a morgue, made them feel more exposed on the empty street outside the hotel. The adjacent shops were all closed, metal shutters down for the night. Their skin, dry from air conditioning, began to moisten in the muggy evening warmth. Following directions given to them by the hotel receptionist, they turned a corner into a dirt road of box-like concrete houses, which smelt of dust and sweat, cologne and sour meat. The front doors were open, and people sat outside on the street, bidding the evening a listless goodbye as Vallenato accordion music wailed from their stereos. Children played or crouched on the concrete floors within, watching television in small rooms partitioned by cheap patterned curtains. After about fifty metres, they found two open-air restaurants, right next to each other and both empty, music blaring from competing sound systems, and sat down at a table looking out over the street. The owner, a tall, big-bellied man with white skin and a moustache, welcomed them with enthusiasm. He took their orders for steak to the kitchen and brought them beer, then slapped his podgy hands down on the table and smiled, wanting to chat. He asked what they were doing in town and Pacho responded, leaning back and looking at him seriously.

"We're journalists. Just working on a story about the situation around here. It looks pretty calm, not as bad as some places."

The big man smiled more broadly.

"Hey," he said, "do you like music? I have Deep Purple, Metallica. Everyone around here likes Vallenato, but you know, I've always liked rock." He nodded to Robert. "Your gringo rock. I've got quite a collection. You guys just tell me what you want and if I've got it I'll put it on."

"Jimmy Hendrix?" asked Robert.

The big man smiled, nodding his head in approval.

"Jimmy Hendrix," he repeated, drawing out the syllables, "Jim-my Hen-drix. No, I haven't got Jimmy Hendrix. It's a shame."

"Then Metallica," said Pacho, beating his fingers on the table in a sudden drum roll, "But not too loud."

The big man bustled back behind the bar, where he had stacks of CDs piled between glinting liquor bottles.

"Look at those guys behind me," said Pacho.

Two men had taken a table in the next restaurant. They had shaven heads and their skinny, fidgety bodies fitted the depressing profile of the typical Colombian contract killer.

"Could be," said Robert.

"They're keeping an eye on us."

"Fuck them," said Robert, but not very loudly. And he laughed and took a swig of beer. "They're not going to do anything," he said.

Pacho sniggered too. They clinked their bottles.

The restaurateur returned, thrusting his belly to the music as he weaved between the empty tables.

"He is good shit, eh?" he said, in English, smiling at Robert. "He is good music. Strong."

"Strong," Robert agreed.

Gradually, the warm night was beginning to seem more pleasant. The stars were bright in the sky above the little jungle town and a couple drove by on a low-powered motorbike, which whined like a mosquito, a bare-footed girl clutching the driver tight around his waist. The fat man wanted to make them feel still more at home and offered to introduce them to some girls.

"No thanks," said Robert, laughing.

"What type of girls?" asked Pacho.

"What do you like? Honey-coloured? Black? White?" Pacho laughed.

"No, don't worry about it," said Robert.

"Things aren't so bad around here," said Pacho, "although we saw a guy who got it this afternoon. Over there."

The restaurant owner lowered his voice.

"I heard about that. He'd sold to the other side. Big mistake."

"Ah," said Pacho, nodding his head. "The other side."

"Big mistake. That doesn't make it pleasant of course."

"No, of course not. But still."

"It's ugly, yes, I admit that."

"Well, yes, but, overall, things seem pretty calm."

It seemed to be the right thing to say. The restaurant owner nodded.

"Life isn't so bad around here these days. It used to be, well, much more difficult."

"When the other side was here?"

"Oh yes. But now, well, it's pretty quiet."

"That's how we're perceiving it. The place is progressing," said Pacho.

"Our guys now, they're the good bad guys. The other guys were the bad bad guys."

Then, more loudly, smiling again, the fat man asked if they wanted another round of beers. He brought them their steaks, which looked as if they'd been hacked off an animal with an axe and were served on wooden platters, together with fried potatoes, fried banana and white rice.

The typical Colombian ultra-carb diet, made palatable by fat. The only small portion was of salad: a dainty saucer of chopped tomato and onion. They ate and drank, feeling now rather cheerful. At some point, they noticed the two men with short haircuts had left. They agreed that it would be advisable to depart themselves at dawn.

There was some sociable evening traffic on the streets now, mostly the whining motorbikes. A smart four-wheel drive with darkened windows pulled up and a tall, slim girl got out and went and sat at the bar, where she started talking to the fat man. The car drove off.

"God, see that?" said Robert.

"Local produce."

Pacho called the fat man over.

"Why don't you introduce us to your friend?"

Their host returned to the bar, and the girl, long-legged and nonchalant, eased herself off the stool with a swivel of her hips. Her face was serious until the moment she joined them at the table and then she smiled, but without showing her teeth.

"Cigarette?" asked Pacho, and she took one and put it in her mouth and they leant towards each other across the table and he lit it. His technique with women was always the same and, despite his house-of-horror looks, it occasionally brought success.

"Have you ever worked as a model?" he said, "I'm a photographer."

"No."

"You should. I could help you."

"No thanks."

"A girl like you, you should be a model. How on earth does such a beautiful girl like you come to live in a place like this?"

"I don't know. I was born."

"I'm sorry, I didn't mean to run down your town."

"It's okay, I don't like it either."

She was looking down at the table, tapping her cigarette in the dented tinfoil ashtray. She really was beautiful. A large mouth in a broad but delicate face, brown eyes, white skin, bobbed hair dyed auburn. She had broad shoulders for a woman, but carried them well.

Robert asked what her name was and she arched her back and shifted in her chair to look at him.

"Milena," she said, smiling again. "What's yours?"

He told her, adding that he was an English journalist, based in Bogota. It was pretty easy for Robert to sound impressive in a town where even the best hotel had no hot water. He asked what she did and she said she studied.

"You know, round here."

"Good place to study?"

She laughed.

"I live here."

Robert had reached the stage where alcohol took over the job of making conversation and it did so inoffensively. In a journalistic sort of way, he asked a series of straight-forward, factual questions, and she seemed to enjoy answer-

23

ing them. This must show he was good-looking, he thought. He wasn't worried about paramilitaries any more. She told him about nearby beaches and said she liked waterskiing. She had been studying law, she said, which sounded unlikely. Anyway, the local college had closed its law course, so she had switched to clothes design. She indicated the pink X-shaped fabric covering her small breasts. She had designed that. She got onto the subject of her family and so he asked about her parents. It was an unexceptional story. Her father had been a coffee farmer near Pereira but had been kidnapped by the guerrillas when she was a little girl. They had paid the ransom but the guerrillas had killed him anyway. They were like that. The family had been forced to leave the farm and move south to the cocaine belt where there was money.

"That's a shame," said Robert.

"Yes, it is a shame," she said, and made a small, self-pitying, affirmative sound. "I never really knew him."

"Why did they kill him?" he asked again.

She shrugged.

"They're bastards."

"Oh dear."

And then she pouted, repeating that slight whimper, drawing the conversation back to herself.

"Poor little me."

Pacho had gone to the bar some time ago to talk to the fat man. But first he had made a contribution to Robert's cause by describing him as a famous war correspondent.

"Why do you work with him?" asked Milena.

"He's my cameraman, and he also takes photos. He's a very good photographer. Very artistic."

"He looks like he's low class."

"He certainly is, but that's part of his charm."

"I don't like the look of him."

"Ah, but I like the look of you."

"Silly."

She took a sip of her beer and asked him if he was married.

"I was," he said, "but journalism isn't a good profession for home life. You're always away. It's like being a sailor. Except without the homosexuality, of course."

Her eyes opened wide.

"She was jealous?"

"No. There was nothing for her to be jealous of."

She smiled again, showing her straight teeth, leaning towards Robert.

"Ah, she got bored?"

"Pretty much. Now I'm married to my job."

"That's terrible."

That pout. One-third joke, one-third sincere, one-third come-on.

A bit later, Robert suggested she accompany him to his hotel.

"We could discuss our hopes and dreams."

"No. My mother wouldn't let me."

"How old are you?"

"Twenty-two."

"So, must be your bed-time."

"Silly. But she'll be waiting up for me now. She'll be worried."

"Twenty-two, eh. Almost as old as me."

"Silly."

"You're right. I'm much, much older than you. I'm very old."

"You're not that old. How old are you?"

"I'm thirty-nine."

"That's not old for a man. That's a good age, it means you're not a boy."

He told her they were leaving tomorrow and asked her to visit him in Bogota. She laughed, but he asked for her phone number and she gave it to him, together with an e-mail address. Then she said her mother was expecting her at home and she went to the bar and made a phone call. Within five minutes the four-wheel drive pulled up outside the restaurant. Robert couldn't see who was driving because of the tinted windows.

"Call me," she said, and kissed Robert on the cheek. She said goodbye to the fat man and to Pacho and got into the car, closing the door quickly behind her.

Pacho shook his head at Robert, grinning.

"You foreigners," he said, "Just like James Bond."

Three

At 4.15 he was woken by a guerrilla who stood by his bivouac and hissed. It was dark and the air was damp and cold, and he balanced a torch on the ground so he could see as he pulled on his jeans and boots, crouching beneath the tarpaulin, which leaked dew when he brushed against it with his forehead.

It had been their second night in the camp. The guerrillas were doing stretching exercises in the dark, clumping in the mud with their cheap rubber boots.

Robert saw Pacho.

"Rested?"

But Pacho only hawked and spat. He lit the day's first cigarette. The jungle was sopping with moisture. Dew dripped noisily from the trees.

"Oh fuck," said Pacho, coughing. "I've got to take a shit."

Robert laughed.

"You'd better go and look for the latrine pit," he said. "Take a torch, don't fall in."

The FARC camp spread over a gently sloping hillside, leading down to the dirt road on one flank and a jungle stream on the other. It included two recently constructed wooden huts, which were used as meeting places, but the guerrillas, perhaps fifty of them, slept in their bivouacs. As a condition of peace talks, the government had temporarily pulled troops out of this territory, and Robert had seen another, much larger, camp a few kilometres along the road, where the rebels had built barracks as well as open-air kitchens and classrooms for lessons in Marxism. These rustic constructions, made of planks, looked at once flimsy and ridiculously picturesque, and on them hung wooden plaques with revolutionary slogans, such as "With Bolivar and the people!" and the famous battle cry of Che Guevara, which sounds so much better in Spanish, *"Hasta la victoria, siempre!"*

Alfredo had returned the previous day, driving noisily into camp in a stolen four-wheel drive, and had told them they might have to wait some time until it was safe before going beyond the demilitarised zone. In his comic, bullying way, he had tried to convince them to accompany his men during an attack on the army. Robert had thanked him and said perhaps on some other occasion.

It was slowly getting light, the jungle taking shape from blackness, turning from grey to green. Pacho came back, a roll of toilet paper sticking out of a pocket and carrying a piece of soap in a smeary plastic bag.

"I'm going down to the river, to wash my hands."

Robert went with him, and they found three guerrillas, two skinny male adolescents and a dumpy young girl, washing in the running water, lathering their brown bodies and shivering. They were still in their underwear and they pushed their hands inside the wet fabric to clean their genitals without exposing them. Rules of modesty were strictly enforced in rebel camps and sexual relations only allowed with a commander's permission.

Robert had not washed since they left the coca-growing town where they had seen the dead man, but his towel and changes of underwear were in his backpack, so he just splashed water over his face and hair. Pacho stripped down to his jocks and waded into the stream. He had a hairless body, thin-armed and heavy-bellied, like a giant, olive-skinned frog's. The young rebels ignored him out of shyness.

A girl brought them breakfast when they returned to their tents: a mess can of sweet coffee made with river water, and another full of rice mixed with thin brown noodles and topped with oily shavings of fried sausage. They ate with appetite, which had seemed to expand with boredom. Meals were the way to mark time in the camp: breakfast at six; lunch at eleven, dinner at four. For an hour after eating they would sit quietly, the day slipping away more quickly thanks to the starch. Robert had brought a book, a rather dull history of Colombia in English. But, although he crawled into his tent with every intention of reading, he found he couldn't keep his eyes focussed for more than a few pages. He couldn't sleep during the day either, and the guerrillas sowed mines around their camps, so walks were inadvisable except along well-beaten trails. Robert hiked into the village on the second day, but the scared look of the local people at the sight of him was discouraging, and the guerrilla sentries, although they did not interfere with him, seemed suspicious of his intentions, so he did not repeat the exercise. Most of his time he spent sitting on a log with Pacho, looking at the trees and trying to think of some new topic of conversation. Pacho, although a committed depressive, was a good talker, fascinated by the violent narrative of his own life. He had grown up in a Medellin slum, and his former childhood playmates had become hitmen or errand boys for drug traffickers before being wiped out in the wars against Pablo Escobar.

"If I hadn't become a photographer, I would be dead too," he had said, stubbing out a cigarette on an ant.

Pacho looked older than his age, which was somewhere in his late thirties, and he walked with a weary, premature stoop, as if his boots were too heavy for him. A smile was always a surprise on his face, although he liked jokes, even Robert's, which he often struggled to understand. His upbringing had given him a bleak and fatalistic outlook, enhanced by a habit of generalisation. One of his favourite subjects was women.

"There are so many in Medellin," he said. "They're just everywhere, looking for you. I don't know why. I suppose it's because so many of the men have been killed."

"That can't be true, statistically," said Robert.

"Brother, it's a fact. You don't realise just how many people have been murdered in Medellin. It's a dangerous place."

"I mean, you might go to places with plenty of girls, but it can't be because there aren't any men."

"All I know is that the girls are out there. Waiting," said Pacho, and he looked Robert in the eyes.

Robert thought about Milena. Back in England, he would never have had a chance with a girl like that.

"She could have been on the cover of *Vogue*," he said, shifting on the log.

"This is true. What a girl. *Qué chica*," said Pacho, and he laughed. "What a night. You were just like James Bond."

Then Robert gave voice to a thought he wanted to get rid of rather than consider.

"You don't think she was a prostitute, do you?"

"You never know," said Pacho.

"But she didn't want to come back with me to my room. Surely, if she'd been a prostitute, she'd have come back with me."

"That's true."

"No, she can't be a prostitute."

One theme to which they returned periodically was that of the subject of their assignment, the FARC's American guerrilla, about whom they knew absolutely nothing. Nonetheless, Pacho felt he had heard enough to form an opinion of the man's personality and motives.

"He must be one of those student types, don't you think," he said, looking around him at the bivouacs pitched in mud, "If he was a girl, he would just have got laid with a Colombian, some immigrant peasant, and that would have been his contribution to the revolution. But he isn't, is he? He's a guy, so he went and actually came down here. The stupid gringo. He'll be regretting it now all right."

"I don't know," said Robert, who tended to agree with Pacho's main point but felt compelled to pay at least casual respects to empathy, "Not everyone's motivations are the same."

And then, to make this clear to Pacho, he said, "I mean, look at priests. Have you ever seen how they live?"

But Pacho laughed, and Robert immediately felt his example was ridiculous.

"Bullshit. This gringo's no priest. Just like Alfredo isn't the Pope."

"Whatever," said Robert, "He's probably regretting it now."

He had no mental image of the guy anyway. He didn't think about him much. He was just a story. And he could never concentrate on stories as well as he would like.

"And, you know what," said Pacho, "This isn't even his country, it isn't his war."

The surrounding jungle didn't provide much entertainment. They never saw an animal, and only very few birds; just insects, especially mosquitoes and flies, which bit them on every part of their bodies, even on their ankles and feet, despite their thick socks and boots, and on their testicles. They sprayed themselves regularly with insect repellant to protect against malaria and leishmaniasis, but it seemed to make no difference to the mosquitoes. Sitting in the heat under the trees in the green light, sticky with sweat, dirty and scratching, Robert thought of cool water and hot showers, of chilled beer and air conditioning, of smooth, clean sheets, and, between them, the sleek Milena.

The guerrillas were just as bored as they were, although more resigned to the camp squalor and lacking any prospect of escape. They slouched about in their baggy uniforms in work details of two or three, digging latrine pits or burying rubbish, or standing guard, chewing shoots of grass. Most of them were very young, some no more than 15, and, while the threat of punishment meant none dodged work, few seemed to do it with enthusiasm. The exception was when a task was related to food. One of the rare occasions when the rebels seemed to enjoy themselves was when, on their first morning in the camp, two guerrillas had appeared dragging a pig by a rope. It broke free, squealing in panic, and the guerrillas laughed and took turns to try to rugby-tackle the animal and snatch hold of its rope. The chase was a celebration of the meal which the pig, soon cornered, quickly became. When the guerrillas weren't occupied with chores, their superiors made sure they were exercising, washing or eating. After nightfall, the camp commander, a mumbling peasant with long, jagged fingernails, called his troops together in one of the huts, where he read them pages of Marxist doctrine, pausing after each sentence to offer an explanation. This he obviously found difficult, and he sounded for all the world like an uninspired Anglican priest stumbling over a sermon.

They were secretive about these evening meetings, and didn't invite Pacho and Robert. By eight o'clock, the rebels were in bed. Every guerrilla always carried a gun. Robert asked a few of them whether they had been in combat and just when exactly they thought the revolution would triumph, but they giggled or turned away. He confused them and made them feel ashamed, and they had not received permission to speak to the journalists.

Alfredo lived at another camp and had designated an assistant to look after them. He was known as Hugo, which was, like all the guerrillas' names, an alias. Hugo was a trim, brown-faced man in his late thirties who was continually stretching his back, as if he wanted to see if he could make himself any taller, and removing his beret to comb his thick black hair. He resented the two visitors, and when Robert spoke to him he affected not to understand his accent, instead turning to Pacho with a grimace to ask what he had said. Silly with boredom, Robert would slap Hugo on the back and smile while he swore at him in English, until the guerrilla became suspicious and threatened violence if he could prove any clear affront.

On the third day, while they were eating breakfast, Hugo appeared before them, wearing a green FARC-made backpack.

"Time to go," he said, turning on his heel as if he was about to march off immediately.

"Wait, we've got to get our stuff," said Robert, adding, in English and in a low voice, "you bastard."

When Robert fetched his backpack, Hugo pointed to one of his assistants.

"He'll carry it. We've got to walk. Guerrillas are used to it, but it'll be hard for you."

But Robert insisted on carrying his own pack.

It began to rain, heavy drops torpedoing through the trees and splashing in streams from the leaves. Robert and Pacho had brought cheap plastic raincoats, essentially sheets with a hooded hole for the head, and slipped them over their packs, so they looked like sodden hunchbacks. Pacho was also carrying the big TV camera, which he had wrapped in a sheet of thick plastic, slung in front of him across his stomach.

Hugo strode in front, walking as fast as he could, as if he particularly wanted to lose Robert and Pacho, who followed with two guides. They headed down to the road, whose dirt ruts were running with channels of water, and continued along it for about a kilometre before turning into the jungle, where the tree canopy closed in on them again above a ridgeway beaten by peasants or animals along the spine of a thickly-grown hill. Slipping and sliding in his rubber boots, Robert tried to keep pace with Hugo, who bent back branches which had grown across the path, hacking them with a machete. But, despite the difficulty of keeping up and of balancing the weight of his pack, it was a pleasure to walk through the jungle, cooled by rain, after the days of inactivity in the guerrilla camp. The trees blocked out the sun above them and the light was filtered through layers of leaves; the only colours were green and red-brown and wet silver. Robert felt small under the high canopy, like a drop of water sliding through grass on someone's enormous lawn. At one point a stream crossed the path, but Hugo, keen to demonstrate his unwavering guerrilla determination, did not hesitate and waded straight through, sinking into the mud almost up to his knees. Robert followed, and the water lapped over the sides of his rubber boots. Once on dry land, hopping on one foot and looking ahead of him to keep an eye on Hugo, he emptied his boots before putting them back on over his soaking socks and hurrying onwards.

They walked for about two hours before they reached the bank of a narrow river, where more guerrillas were waiting for them by a long canoe-shaped motor boat, pulled up on the mud.

Robert, feeling jaunty, turned to Pacho.

"How's it going?" he asked.

Pacho's face was purple and pink. His blondish hair stuck limply to his wet forehead beneath the grey plastic of his rain-sheet hood. He clutched the hump on his stomach where he held his camera like a heavily pregnant woman, breathing with his mouth open.

"We're going in a fucking boat? That's just what we need, more water," he said.

Small mosquitoes danced in the dank air under the trees, and Robert took aerosol repellent from a pocket on his backpack, spraying his whole body, including his clothes, beneath the plastic sheet. Hugo shooed them towards the water, saying they had to hurry, and Robert swore.

The guerrilla in charge of the boat pushed it into the water and they sat side by side on a wet metal bench, arranging themselves beneath their dripping plastic sheets. Hugo sat in front of them, next to two young women who were coming along to help them make camp. Their pilot yanked the cord of the outboard motor and steered them into the river, which curved through thick jungle, the banks close together so that trees sometimes overlapped above them, branches trailing into the water. They picked up speed, the front of the boat lifting up, and the drizzling rain became a constant spray, making them shiver beneath their sheets, and they had to be on their guard against low-lying branches which whipped against their faces and had to be fended off with their hands. The guerrilla at the motor steered standing up, a small machine gun slung across his back, his dark, high-cheekboned, moustached face expressionless. Robert had flown above jungle like this in an army helicopter, and knew that they were virtually invisible from the air; all any passing soldiers would see would be tree tops and the yellow-brown veins of hundreds of Amazon tributaries, occasionally glinting when the sun pushed through the clouds. At one point, branches hung over the river so thickly and so low that they had to cut the motor and use their hands to pull the boat forward through the trees, leaning back until they were free and could accelerate again, quickly reaching full speed. They were feeling cold now, and Pacho produced a hipflask from somewhere beneath his folds of plastic, passing it to Robert. "First class," said Pacho, and Robert, taking a swig of whisky, responded, with a smile, "First class." For a moment, filthy and trembling, they were like two irresponsible schoolboys on a camping excursion, and Robert felt he didn't want to meet the American guerrilla after all, he wanted to push back work and responsibility, he wanted to watch the jungle shores whizz by from a boat. He saw a thick python coiled on a riverside branch, a tempter taking his ease in a pathless Eden. A fantastic, crested bird with a long beak took flight, like something out of an early illustration of the New World, painted from the description of a conquistador. Pacho twisted around and offered the whisky to the guerrilla steering the boat, and he took it with a smile, but without slowing down.

They stopped some time in the late afternoon, pulling up alongside jungle which to Robert was indistinguishable from the thickly tree-lined shores they had been passing for hours. But once they disembarked, stiff, sopping and cold, they saw the signs of previous guerrilla presence: wooden platforms made of planks, collapsing and uneven from decay, where they could hoist tarpaulins and make their beds, and a pit topped with ashes.

Hugo began chopping wood to prepare a fire.

"Don't offer to help, let him do it," said Pacho. But Robert took his turn with the hatchet, chipping away the black, soaked outer layers of a log to expose light-coloured wood which was still dry. He worked with vigour but wasn't very good at it, and Hugo, who had been standing behind him all the time, afraid he would do it well, smiled in petty triumph and took the hatchet back. Pacho laughed, jigging up and down with his knees to keep warm and sheltering a cigarette with his hands.

The two girl guerrillas started the fire under the drizzle and they crowded as close as they could to warm their wet clothes. It was beginning to get dark, the tangled trees, the sky, the slippery river banks and the water itself all merging into the same wet blackness, as if slipping gently beneath the opaque ooze of a slowly rising swamp. Only the flames were visible, and the shivering faces crowded around them. The women, who were both perhaps twenty years old, had brought pots and pans from the canoe, as well as maize flour, salt and soup powder, and they fried arepas. The maize pancakes, usually tasting of insipid dough, had a delicious, fatty taste on that chilly night, and they served them with mess cans of hot soup. Once they had eaten, the guerrillas began to talk. Robert didn't understand much of what was being said, but the well-fed, low sound of it was pleasant to hear in the firelight, surrounded by jungle. The girls, who were not good-looking but slim and not unattractive, suggested they play cards, but Robert wanted to sleep. They had already prepared their tents, slung with mosquito nets above the slimy wooden platforms, and he used his torch to find his toothbrush in his backpack and then felt his way to the steep muddy riverbank where he leant down by the black water. Then he took off his wet jumper and jeans, rubbed himself, shivering, with a smelly towel, and put on dry clothes. He crawled into his sleeping bag, laid beneath his tarpaulin, which was pitched low to keep the wind out, and felt snug. It was absolutely dark and he was lying on planks right by the river. He listened to the splashing sounds of the water and later a sudden rush of rain and the unidentifiable sounds of the jungle and he thought of the snake he had seen earlier, coiled around a branch, and hoped none would slide into his sleeping bag. He felt he was lost in the world somewhere, deep in the dark jungle and when, later that night, he heard the sound of an aeroplane droning high overhead, it was a strange, threatening sound and he hoped that whoever it was did not know where they were and could not find them.

Four

They woke him very early. Their story had been delivered by river. He pulled off his dry t-shirt and pants and put on the clammy clothes he had used the day before. Then he pushed his feet into his rubber boots, which farted with yesterday's water. It was still too dark to see, but he could feel mist chilling his cheeks.

"Coffee?"

Pacho said, "Not yet. They'll have to light a fire first."

"You all ready?"

"Yes."

He found his tape recorder and the notebook with a biro pushed through its binding rings. His fingers were clumsy and sore. Birds were singing. It was dawn now, the first, slow-developing black-and-white photograph of morning

"The fire?"

"The girls will start it," said Pacho, spitting.

Then they saw what they had come to see. The gringo was standing by the flooded remains of the previous night's fire and looked up when he heard them coming. Two other guerrillas had arrived with him, but it was the American's expression that gave away his identity. He looked uncom-

41

fortable, self-conscious in his combat gear, caught out in some unspecified act of sin. Otherwise it would have been hard to tell him apart from the Colombians. He was short and sallow-skinned. Robert, trying to gather his thoughts for the interview as he hauled himself through the mud, was disappointed, and he knew Pacho, with his photographer's eye for the self-explanatory image, must feel the same.

The gringo said nothing. But he had found a way to look at them. He was more confident now, disdainful even. He raised his face, which was round and framed by a beret and a scant beard, and stared. It was a big angry black man's stare in a small white man's face, as if Robert's very presence was offensive. His companions stood by him, seeing Robert more than looking at him, their eyes blank, ready for any expression.

An interview, he had always thought, isn't really like a conversation, although that's a common misconception. If it's good, it's more like rape. Robert extended his hand.

"Hi," he said, pronouncing his name.

A bad start. As if his identity meant anything. As if he was the point of the exercise. The American maintained his defensive cool, looking up at Robert, whose height was clearly an additional insult. But the use of English, just its sound, seemed intimate, as if the Colombians all around them had slipped from focus.

"You're a Brit?"

"Yeah."

"Martín."

He pronounced it in the Spanish way, with a strong R and stressing the final syllable. His hand was small and plump.

"That's not your real name."

He smiled. It is always complimentary to be associated with mystery.

"Can you tell me your real name?"

"Of course not."

"Of course."

Black stare, white face. Robert explained he was a reporter, even though this must have been obvious.

"Journ-a-list," said Martín, stringing out the syllables.

He looked away, his lips pursed, nodding slowly. They were standing around the mess left by last night's fire. The camp place was just a muddy gash in the jungle.

Robert's head had yet to settle. He wiped his eyes, still itchy with sleep. He had to struggle to concentrate. It seemed so quiet, despite the noise of birds, the sound of seeping water.

"We just want to speak to you for a while, about what you're doing here, why you're here," he said. But these words, so routine, so professional, sounded flat and in-appropriate. He felt the American would have been grate-ful for something more emotional, for something to mark the occasion, even some recognition of something, a recog-nition, perhaps, of suffering. But Robert wasn't up to that, it was too complicated.

He rubbed his tingling hands.

"People are going to be very interested in you, back in the United States," he said.

Martín was looking at him with that fake indifference again, that mannered disdain. This is so much more important to him than it is to me, thought Robert. And how could it be otherwise? Their meeting was extraordinary and mundane at the same time.

"What you want is just gossip, it's entertainment."

"No, it's not. I work for serious publications," said Robert.

"They're all the same shit."

Maybe, he thought, just maybe. His mouth was dry. So he proposed they have a cup of coffee and looked around to see if the girls were properly roused and preparing to brew up. He wanted the gringo to cool it a bit. But then the guy began to shout.

"Hey, no photos. I didn't say you could take photos."

He was yelling in Spanish. His accent was irregular, with gringo diphthongs, the give-away wavering "oh" sound. Robert wondered how much he could really understand the Colombians he was living with.

"*Tranquilo, hermano, tranquilo*" said Pacho. "Take it easy, brother."

He lowered his still camera, screwing on the lens cap.

"I've got my security to consider," said Martín, in English.

This could be a problem, Robert thought. They needed

those images. But the guy was also sounding more of an American now, with personal preoccupations, priorities. In an instant he had lost some of his poise, his white man's borrowed negritude.

"No one knows I'm here, man," said Martín, and a bird high in the tree canopy, invisible from their small stretch of mud on the riverbank, began a long, percussive cry, a repetitive sound like a drum, something hard striking something hollow. He looked in his mid-twenties. That was predictable. And Robert felt sorry for the guy, for the kid.

Pacho offered cigarettes all round. Martín and his two companions took several each. So did the two girls, the boatman and Hugo, who had been unhappy about the conversation in a foreign language and touched Pacho on the shoulder.

"He says we've got to go soon," said Pacho.

Robert looked round to see if he could catch Hugo's eye, but he had slunk away. The girls were starting a fire anyway. Martín turned towards the river, slightly raising one shoulder as he smoked to keep his rifle strap from slipping.

Then Robert thought of all the time, all the money he had put into the trip and, for the first time, he was afraid it could be wasted. Fear banished sympathy from his mind. Two thousand words, he thought, that's all I need, you little shit. A few photographs and ten minutes of edited interview on video. This guy's getting worked up over ten minutes of video. He thinks he's such a big deal.

"Hey, I've got something for you," he said, and went back to his tent, digging in his backpack for the crushed remains of his present, wrapped in a plastic bag. "I'm sorry, but I'm afraid they've probably melted."

Martín took the package and laughed.

"Hershey bars. Fucking Hershey bars. Shut up. You've got to be kidding."

"And, in case you're out of touch," said Robert, handing him a few crumpled copies of *Time* magazine. "Well, just in case."

"That shit. Thank you anyway."

He stuffed the chocolate into one of the large pockets of his camouflage trousers. The magazines remained dangling from one hand.

Robert had his mind on the job now. The guy had to be prompted to talk, to be made to relax.

"So what did you do back in the States? Were you at university, at college, or something?"

Martín clucked his tongue in warning. "Oh, no you don't," he said. But he asked who they were working for, and nodded when he heard the names, breathing out smoke as he looked at his rubber boots.

"It was very difficult to get here, you know," said Robert.

"Sure, I know."

"And, as you're probably aware, we have Alfredo's permission to speak to you. He said you'd speak to us. He set the whole thing up and sent us with guides. That's why we're here."

46

"They could hassle my family if they knew I was here," said Martín.

But Robert said, "Come on, I assume they live in the U.S.A. What could they possibly do to them?"

Martín shook his head, smiling with his mouth shut. His face was podgy and ill-defined, but his eyes, slightly slanted, were what you mainly remembered about it, because of their timing, the precise moments at which they looked at you. His wispy beard didn't suit him. It just made him appear dirty and adolescent.

"Do? They can do lots of stuff."

His smile had got stuck, and he turned his face away. His gun strap slipped on one of his round shoulders, so he had to hoist it up again.

Robert said, "All I want to do is talk to you about why you think what you're doing is important."

The word "important" had seemed heavy on his tongue.

"And it is important, that's true. Yeah."

It was fully light now. The girls were making breakfast.

Martín said, "And what are you doing anyway? Why is what you're doing important?"

This guy will speak to me out of vanity, thought Robert. It was the James Dean factor, the Che Guevara factor, those good-looking corpses and their baneful influence. This guy is a rebel, so he'll want to look like one. He first wanted to be a rebel because he saw them on TV. So you've got to be on TV if you want to be a rebel, even if it's just to scowl and say the media's crap. There's no point just sitting in the jungle

47

where nobody can see you. He's got to speak to me, because the media created him. It's like the monster who simply has to have his chat with Dr. Frankenstein.

"I just want to report what you say," he said. And then he added, "And I'm here because Alfredo wants me to be here."

Martín trod his cigarette butt into the mud and exhaled: a long, shuddering, smokeless exhalation.

"Let's go sit down. I need to sit down. We were on that boat all night."

They could smell the smoke from the fire. There was going to be coffee. The smell of the smoke blended with the smells of leaves and mud. The other guerrillas were leaving them alone. They didn't understand what they were saying anyway. Pacho had withdrawn to allow Robert to work on Martín. They sat on a log by the river, looking at the jungle on the other side, just ten metres away. The American fidgeted in his fatigues. Robert was silent.

"You know," said Martín, presently, "I believe that all revolutionaries are guided by great feelings of love."

Okay, here we go, thought Robert. But he had a hollow feeling, as if this was something he had done before and it was easy but he wasn't interested in it any more.

"That's a quote. I didn't think of that, it's from Che Guevara," said Martín.

"Che Guevara?" said Robert. It was funny.

The American looked at him.

"Do you get what I mean? Do you get that?"

"Yeah, I think so."

Robert put his tape recorder on the log, switched off, next to his notebook. He wanted Martín to speak on camera, but first he just had to begin speaking, to get going. People like to talk anyway, to objectify themselves.

"Can I ask why you first became so interested in Colombia?"

This was really the key question, even if no one else cared. What was this guy's justification, what was his excuse for himself? But Martín took it at face value.

"Oh, but man, once you find out about what's going on here, once you read about it, it just makes you want to weep."

Robert had heard about it all before. But he would have been pleased for Martín to repeat it on tape. Quietly, he said, "But love doesn't necessarily make you take a gun, does it? There are other ways of helping people."

Martín shook his head. He smiled.

"Every time the people try to get what's theirs, they kill them."

Robert spoke carefully.

"Most people wouldn't do what you do," he suggested. "I don't agree with you, but I can see it's admirable in a way. You've made sacrifices. You've given up a lot, haven't you?"

"I have, yes."

The young American's voice had shrunk. It was lonely out here in the jungle. He paused, considering, and then he spoke more strongly again, with an enthusiasm which struck Robert as borrowed.

"But you know, once you get here, you realise that it's about more than just you. You're part of the struggle. Everyone's in it together, and they share what they've got, and they just don't complain, man, they don't complain. You feel happy. Hey, do you see what I mean?"

Robert nodded. Of course he saw what he meant.

"I don't think the armed struggle's the answer," he said.

Martín smiled. "That's utopian, man. You're a liberal."

Mist rose from the brown river. Grey clouds hung low in the sky and the jungle on the far bank was dark green. One of the girls brought them coffee. It was always the women who served food.

"Why Colombia, Martín? Why the FARC?"

The guerrilla laughed, and shook his head, looking away again. Then he repeated Robert's question.

"Why the FARC? Why Colombia?"

"Yeah, why not help poor people in the States, or refugees in Africa? Why Colombia, why did you choose here?"

"Well it doesn't matter, does it? Because here I am. It's a fact."

"I suppose I'm here too, but then I'm being paid."

That was Robert's reason, and it was as good as any. Then Martín gave his crazy convinced smile again, the thought-proof evangelical leer.

"You're a tool, man, you're a tool of the media establishment."

Robert said, "Does your family know you're here?"

50

Martín smiled again. His grin just lasted too long.

"The revolution isn't personal," he said.

"Okay."

Chill time. Almost time to pop the question. But you've got to amble into it. So Robert asked him about his rifle, which Martín unslung and held out.

"AK47."

"Of course. Russian made?"

"I think this one's from China, they make them everywhere now, they're copies."

"So, what's it like living with these guys, in a camp?"

But Martín was concentrating on his coffee. One of the day's principal pleasures. His head was disproportionately large for his narrow-shouldered body, like a child's. He pushed back his beret, exposing the curly dark hair above his pale, sweaty forehead.

"Listen, Martín, can we speak to you on camera? All you have to do is to talk about exactly the same things we've been talking about now. Just for about twenty minutes."

The timing had seemed right. But Martín said, "No, I don't think so."

Robert said, "Alfredo wants you to talk."

"I'll talk. Yeah, I like you. But not on camera."

Robert rubbed his face. Then he pushed his hands back through his hair. He had to rouse himself.

"Without a camera it's just not the same. Martín, come on, do me a favour."

If you really, really like me, he thought.

Martín smiled.

"It's not about favours, man, you've got to understand me. I like you. But I just can't talk on camera."

And he smiled again.

They did the interview without the camera. Robert held his tape recorder and felt blank. Then they shook hands. Martin was still smiling. Robert and Pacho got into the canoe with the guerrillas and sat together on the cold metal bench. As the canoe pulled away into the yellow river, he looked back at the young American on the shore and watched until their progression hid him from view behind the trees. Then, for a brief moment, he felt as if he was abandoning him, but not for long, because this was ridiculous, and so he thought of something else, starting with failure. And then he was just tired.

Five

Often in the mornings in Bogota there is a perfect blue sky, but the altitude is too great for it to be hot and it is always cool in the shade, although the equatorial sun burns anyway, so it is a deceitful cool blue, a radiation blue. In the afternoon, fat grey clouds roll in from the hot lowlands over the pine-covered high mountains and dump frozen tropical rain in torrents on the city, where they have built the kerbs high so the water doesn't rush the pavements and the drains are extra broad but clog up with leaves. There are almost no cockroaches, and you don't sweat unless you run, and you can wear a jacket. There are a lot of buildings made of red brick, and scrappy buses, driven by the devil himself, belch soot and roar like explosions in a quarry. The people are refrigerated South Americans, courteous if flashy in the rich quarters but made stand-offish by the European climate of the Andean mountains. You can tell how good a restaurant is by the number of bodyguards waiting outside, leaning on four-wheel drives with darkened windows. They wear suits, have plump, dull faces, and manicured hands. The city seems far away from most of Colombia, but there are a lot of beggars on the streets, and family groups of refugees from the fighting. Many of them have wooden carts, some with drooping, mangy horses, others drawn by human muscle, and the cart people sort through rubbish and just beg on the side. Black women from northern Colombia sell plastic bags and beg at traffic lights with their babies, who play and have plaited hair.

Robert lived alone and so he went out a lot. He never ate in his apartment, because he liked to get out and watch people. But, while he knew a few other foreign reporters, he usually ate alone. So he varied where he ate, not so much because of the food, but because he became bored of the same faces. Often, in bars, he would sit alone before a lovely succession of drinks and look at the girls. But he also had a friend he would drink with.

"There are some days," said his friend Luke, "when you've just got to pay for it."

It didn't sound so bad coming from him. He was a good-looking guy still in his twenties and women usually noticed him. They had just left a nightclub where groups of pretty girls had been standing with groups of pretty boys without dancing. They all wore light-tinted, wrap-around sunglasses and you could only suppose they were enjoying their drugs.

They got into a taxi and headed for a place where, Luke said, the girls dressed like geishas. The driver knew where it was, but when they pulled up by the ordinary-looking house on a quiet, residential street he said the authorities had closed it down.

"Stupid fucker," said Luke. He asked the driver if he

could recommend somewhere else, but decided to try another place he knew when he heard the reply. "He took us there even though he knew it was closed, the idiot. I'll be fucked if I'm going to pay him his full fare."

"So he made a mistake," said Robert.

"It's just so typical."

They'd shared two bottles of wine with dinner before going to the nightclub, where they followed up with beer, and were both quite drunk. The taxi pulled up outside the brothel. Its oddly bland Anglophone name, "El nuevo Manchester", shone in purple neon, and several large men were standing beneath a streetlamp.

"Fuck you, son of a bitch. Motherfucker." said the taxi driver, in English. But the bouncers recognised Luke and ushered him inside. "Motherfucker," repeated the taxi driver.

They descended some steps from the pavement level. It was even darker down there than on the street. Green and purple lights glowed from somewhere behind the bar and from an empty dance floor next to a spiral staircase, made of metal, which led up to the bedrooms. There were a couple of television screens showing very close-up pornography but no one was watching. They sat down on sofas facing each other across a low table and a short, unsmiling middle-aged man in a suit brought them beer.

"Do you think it's safe to drink here?" asked Robert, taking a sip. He wondered what the place would look like if, in some cataclysm perhaps, daylight should break through.

"I suppose the drinks might occasionally be spiked.

Scopolamine. Best be careful," said Luke, also drinking.

Some girls were sitting at the next sofa. Occasionally one would look round to see if she could catch Robert's eye. Luke was facing in the wrong direction. The girls smiled in a tired, knowing way, narrowing their eyes but looking as though they could still see some joke to it all. One of them got up and came over, smoothing down her mini skirt. She was older than the rest, perhaps in her mid-thirties, and was lean and muscular with dyed-blond hair and a strong jaw. She sat next to Robert, rubbing up to him with her thigh.

"*Hola,*" she said.

"*Hola,*" said Robert.

Luke, leaning back in the sofa and smoking, said, "The other place is much better. Much classier, much prettier women."

"Have you been often?"

Robert had never gone with a prostitute himself. He'd often felt like it, but he'd never done it. His friend was immediately defensive.

"Oh, a few times. I don't think there's anything wrong in going to a brothel. Let's face it, sometimes you need sex and your girlfriend is having a period or is in a stink, or you just don't want to go through all the hassle of talking and saying that, yes, you love her, darling, and you want to get married and all that crap. It's a commercial transaction, nice and clean."

"Clean if you wear a condom."

"That, I admit, is a disadvantage."

"What's he saying?" asked the prostitute, placing her hand on Robert's knee.

Luke continued.

"Some guys get really addicted to brothels. Juancho now, you know Juancho Molinos, he'd go all the time. He became obsessed with one girl in particular, the poor idiot. Really got a bit embarrassing. I had to follow him around to make sure he didn't get into trouble."

"And his wife's good-looking. Nice girl as well," said Robert, "This one's making me uncomfortable."

"Tell her to go away. Get another one."

Robert turned to the woman, who was rubbing his upper thigh. She blinked and smiled.

"Where are you from?" she asked.

"We're both English."

"Ah. I used to live in Germany."

"Really? Well, that's very similar. Were you doing this when you were there?"

"Yes. I've only come back for a few months, to renew my visa. I'm going back. I've got a German boyfriend."

Luke said, "Just tell her to go away."

He wasn't looking at any of the girls himself. Maybe he felt constrained by Robert's presence.

The woman didn't have to be told to leave. Robert turned back to his beer and she went to sit with the others without any sign of having taken offense.

"I'd feel bad about sleeping with a prostitute," said Robert. "I'd feel bad for the girl."

Luke shrugged, and then leant forward to tap his cigarette in the ash tray.

"So, you'd prefer they weren't paid?"

"I just can't believe they can be happy sleeping with guys for money. I just don't think people are capable of that."

"People are capable of all sorts of things."

"That's true," said Robert, who was looking at another girl, a pretty one this time. She caught his eye a first time and then looked around again to make sure he was interested.

"Particularly in this country. You can buy anyone here. There's been a moral decay. It's drugs, it's killing, it's women selling themselves. The brothels of Spain are full of Colombians. Why Colombians? Why not Ecuadoreans? Why not Kenyans? Okay, Nigerians, yes, but, there are plenty of people from other poor countries who don't whore themselves nearly as much as Colombians do. It's for a reason. People here are just prepared to do anything for cash. The place is warped."

"You're not going to go with any of these girls?" asked Robert.

"No, I don't think so. I just want a smoke and a beer. I just find a brothel a relaxing place to have a smoke and a beer."

The girl came over and sat by Robert. She was very good looking, and he was surprised at how untouched she looked.

"What's your name?"

"Lucia."

It wasn't real, of course. It was a nom de guerre. Like "Martín".

"What's yours?" she asked.

He noticed her jeans were embroidered with flowers around the part where they flared. However long she'd been here, she still hadn't lost her cute appeal, the appeal to whatever it is, the fatherly instinct, the big-brotherly instinct, the incestuous instinct to protect.

"Why do you do this?" he asked, and then he added, with beery logic, "You're such a pretty girl."

He always found it easy to ask questions. He was a journalist, after all. But even so he was often surprised at how readily people talk about themselves, even about the hardest things, the things which should be most upsetting. This time, he should have controlled himself, out of consideration for Luke, who eased back in his sofa, having decided to concentrate on smoking and drinking.

"Money," she said. "I haven't got any money."

"There must be other ways to make money. Get a job in an office or something. It might not earn you as much but it'd be less unpleasant."

"Oh, it's not that easy. There aren't any jobs. And I haven't got any qualifications."

And she placed a cigarette in her nicely-formed, painted lips and lit it. Only later did it occur to Robert that his questions were probably not unusual to her. He was just an example of a recurring type of sentimental client. Being sad with him was part of her job.

"You should study. Or something. Anything."

"I'd like to study. I wish I could."

"Isn't there any way?"

"I can't. I send money back to my family in Pereira."

"Do they know what you're doing?"

"They don't ask any questions."

The girl touched his thigh.

Robert said to Luke, "She seems a nice girl. What the hell is she doing here?"

Luke made a suggestion.

"If you like her, you could ask her out. Ask for her phone number. You don't have to go with her here. It's very depressing in those cramped little rooms, and it's perfectly okay to ask a prostitute to have, say, lunch with you, if you like her. She might like to see you again too, in more agreeable surroundings."

"Do you think so?"

"Yes, why ever not? Management won't mind. It's good for business."

And he asked her to get a pen and a piece of paper.

"Would you like to come to lunch some time? Maybe I could give you a call," said Robert. She was so pretty and she seemed quite nice.

She looked nervous, but she was smiling. She called over the silent waiter and got a pen from him.

"What's your number?" Robert asked.

"Where I live I don't have a telephone, or I can't use it. But you give me yours."

"Can you call me tomorrow? Let's have lunch."

"Yes, yes, I'd love to."

He wrote down his mobile number, but she frowned.

"It's difficult for me to call a mobile. But I will, some-how."

"Shall we go?" he asked Luke.

"All set up? Good. There's absolutely nothing wrong with taking one of these girls to lunch. Much more enjoy-able than doing anything here."

Robert turned to the girl.

"It was really nice to meet you."

"It was nice to meet you."

Then she smiled, and added, "There's only one thing. You wouldn't be able to help me with just one thing, would you? For the taxi home? Just whatever you can spare."

He gave her a twenty-thousand-peso note.

"Thanks very much."

She kissed him on the cheek. Obviously twenty thou-sand was quite a lot.

"Pretty girl," said Luke when they were outside on the street.

"Yeah. I don't know if I did the right thing."

"Oh, of course you did. I've done just the same. It's been a while though."

"And how did it turn out?"

"Enjoyable enough. You don't have to spend the rest of your life with her. Just have a dirty weekend. That's the good thing about whores. Take her out to lunch and you don't have to pay for anything else. She'll enjoy herself too. It'll be an outing for her."

The night air was cool after the close atmosphere of the underground brothel and there was a full moon in the clear sky. Robert decided to walk home to burn off some of the alcohol. Luke, suave but bulky in a tan overcoat, yelled at a taxi and then climbed in. They agreed to see each other again soon.

He walked fast, his hands in the pockets of his leather jacket, remembering, although he was drunk, to keep his eyes open for whoever else might be around. It was a chilly night and the cold light of the streetlamps was very similar in quality to the glow of the moon, in the way it sucked out colour. Tree tops and the edges of buildings were as sharply defined in black and white as a woodcut. As he walked, the prospect of meeting the girl grew in erotic charge. It was the idea that, after lunch, he could suggest that they go to a hotel. She could hardly be shocked. He wondered if she would ask for payment. He would offer it, but would she accept, he wondered. Maybe it would be more fun if she did accept.

Later, lying in bed, he thought of the girl and how she would ring him in the morning and they would have lunch and then go to a hotel. They wouldn't go to his house, because that might be dangerous, it would be foolish to give a prostitute his address. She was cute in a different way in his thoughts now. Drifting closer to sleep, buoyed and lapped by a muzzy wooze of alcohol, she led him tip-toeing up the spiral staircase to the musty room where he would take his turn with her like all the rest.

The next day he woke early with a washed-out, border-line hangover feeling. He would have liked to have slept more. He felt bloated and loose-skinned, as if someone had pulled off his hide and flapped it like a mat.

He had a shower and went into the kitchen, and then he sat down at the dining room table and drank several cups of strong tea. But he still felt very weary. His eyes fixed on a framed photograph of his daughter, taken at her playschool in London when she was four years old. There was nothing else to look at in the flat, which he rented furnished but which was still pretty bare. It had never occurred to him to add any decorations of his own, except for the photograph. The flat was in good shape but his landlord was an old man and it was fitted out in a heavy, old-fashioned way, with bulky, dark-brown wooden furniture. It was on the ground floor, and, because it was surrounded by trees and other apart-ment buildings, it had a slightly dank, subterranean feel, like a cave.

He turned off his cellphone to avoid the prostitute's call and went for a walk. It was Sunday and the sky was blue. He felt better as he walked, and he headed through the Parque del Virrey, which has a canal to relay water from the moun-tains, and past the walled residences of the French and British ambassadors and went to the Centro Andino shop-ping centre, where he sat down at a café and had an espresso and read *El Tiempo*. Then, after he had used up some time, he went to Tower Records and bought the week-end *Financial Times* from a week earlier and headed out of the shopping center to walk around a bit until lunch. He wore a baseball cap against the sun, and strolled up to Usaquén, along a busy highway which was largely closed off for bicycles on Sundays, and past a military base, and went to an Italian restaurant frequented by the wealthy and by Bogota's few foreigners. The waiter recognised him and shook his hand and brought him a glass of Chilean red wine without his having to ask for it. As he ate, he read articles in the FT about food and buying expensive houses. After lunch he had two more espressos. He felt bad about the girl, but relieved, as if he had asked someone else to do something cruel for him as a favour.

Six

On Monday, he took out his notebook and found Milena's e-mail address, and sent her a note suggesting she come and visit him in Bogota. What the hell, he thought. But he couldn't get out of his mind the memory of how, at the restaurant, she had arrived so soon after the fat man had asked if they wanted to meet girls, and how she had come over as soon as they had asked her to, and how she had been dropped off by a four-wheel drive, and that it had picked her up without the driver showing his face.

She replied within hours.

Robert,

How exciting to see your mail!!!!! I thought you had forgotten about me, a poor little girl in a country town. I was so sad you hadn't contacted me, with not even a phone call. How nice you are. But, we saw each other for such a little time. I don't know what to think. I don't know what I feel.

A kiss,
Milena

He was happy with the fact that he got a reply. He wasn't interested in her for her prose style. He wrote back that he could remember her face, that he could remember her hair. Confusion was natural, he wrote, but what counts is to resolve it, and then he stated that, yes, he was sure of his offer, and added a practical request for personal details so he could buy her an air ticket. And in fact he could remember her face. Human beauty is never original, it's more like a perfect copy, a mathematically exact alignment of the tissues that never lasts but is always repeated.

He had to talk to Pacho about paying him for the trip, so he called him in Medellin.

Pacho had a way of asking for slightly more than was due to him. But Robert liked him and didn't want to make a fuss, so he consented fairly easily. After they had sorted out the money issue they were still on friendly terms, so Robert said, "Hey, you remember that pretty girl we met in that paramilitary town?"

"The day that guy got his head blown off?"

"Yes, that's the one."

"Of course. A very pretty girl. Snotty though. It's probably good we didn't get too friendly with her, she's probably with some paramilitary and that would be dangerous. Why?"

"She wants to come and visit me."

Pacho laughed, that harsh cackle of which Robert was so fond.

"Just like James Bond," Pacho said.

"First class, eh?"

"First class. She called you?"

66

"We've been in contact," said Robert. "It looks like she wants to come and spend the weekend."

"She is very, very good-looking."

"Hey, Pacho, she was probably a whore don't you think? The way she just arrived in that car. It was a bit suspicious, don't you think?"

"I think she probably is."

"Shit, so what do I do with her?"

"You make love to her. What else do you do with her?"

"Yes, obviously." But then he said, "You know Pacho, I don't think she is a whore."

Robert took a beer from his fridge, which contained nothing else besides milk, butter and bread. After drinking it, he had another. It was about lunchtime and he didn't have any particularly pressing work to do, no deadlines to meet. Things couldn't be too bad if girls like Milena were offering themselves to him. He thought about her e-mail, about how she had said she had been confused, that she wasn't sure what she felt about him. A whore wouldn't write that.

In the evening, he checked his inbox, and there, wedged between the spam, was a second reply from Milena. He opened it with confidence but this time it was all wrong. The answer was, although reluctantly, although flirtatiously, no.

He took his notebook from his desk, found her number and called it on his mobile, then took a swig of beer and leant forward on his chair as it rang, placing the bottle on the floor by his feet. It's obvious, after all, he thought. A girl as pretty as she is doesn't go unnoticed in a shitty place like that.

A woman's voice answered and he asked for Milena. He imagined the important sound the telephone must make in the sort of bare, concrete-brick type of house Milena must live in, and of course his foreign accent was in itself a badge of rank.

"Hello?"

"Milena, it's Robert."

She didn't sound as sad as she had said she was in her e-mail. She didn't speak as she wrote at all. She was more confident and in control and definitely not sobbing. But she did seem happy to hear from him. It was only the second time they had ever spoken, but, because of the e-mails, their voices naturally adopted a hushed, intimate inflection.

"I'm so surprised you've called me," she said.

He wondered if that could possibly be true. But it sounded good.

"Why? You didn't want me to?"

"No, I mean, of course I wanted you to. How are you? How have you been?"

"I'm sad," he said.

"Sad. Oh no. Because of me? Why?"

Sometimes she had a Marilyn-Monroe, little-me, little-girl way of speaking. It was flattering, because it was an attempt to soothe in a showy way, it was like a verbal caress and meant to reassure him of his own importance.

"Because you don't want to come and see me."

"Oh no, that's not true. Of course I want to come."

"And you're sad too, so you say."

"Oh, I'm so sad. Don't you believe me?" she said.

"Then why don't you come?"

"I'd love to."

"Good. When? I'll book your ticket right away."

"But Robert, you don't understand. I can't. You know."

Robert assumed her mother or sisters were in earshot.

"Oh, please, I'll be so sad if you don't come," he said, playing her game. And then he added, "We could have a great time, and, I promise you, I am, as I said in my mail, a gentleman, so I'd respect you absolutely. We'd go to restaurants – there are some very nice restaurants in Bogota – to clubs, whatever you like."

"You're such a darling."

"I want to see you again."

"And I want to see you again."

She had lowered her voice.

"Look, I'll put you up in a hotel. Your mother couldn't complain about that, could she? I'd go and visit you, but, you understand, it's not very easy for me down there, for security reasons, and if you come here you would get to see Bogota as well."

"Of course."

"So, you'll come?"

"Oh," she said, drawing out the single syllable into a cat-like stretch of pretty indecision.

"You know, I don't even know your surname," he said.

69

"I've got to have that to book the flight and the room."

"All right," she said, quickly, and he could hear her breathing over the phone. "It's Marulanda, my full name is Ana Milena Marulanda Gomez."

Now that she had said yes he wanted to end the phone call as soon as possible in case she changed her mind. What a beautiful name, he said.

"How about Friday? Friday? Why don't you come on Friday?"

"I'll go on Friday."

"I'm really looking forward to seeing you," he said, and he made sure that it was he who was sounding emotional now.

He had written her details down and, in some vague, voodoo way, he felt he possessed her spirit on that piece of paper. He chuckled in triumph and swigged his beer. Then he stood up. It was too late to make the bookings, but he had to do something, so he washed his face, put on his heavy leather jacket and left his apartment to go and look for dinner.

He was absolutely sure she was not a whore.

Seven

"So, keeping busy?"

"I'm a freelancer. I can't afford not to keep busy."

"Yeah. That sounds like a good scoop of yours."

"Thanks very much. I'm still scratching my mosquito bites."

"Aren't they the worst thing? You can get this sort of gel for that at a pharmacy. It's anaesthetic. It makes those little bumps go numb so they don't itch."

The press flak led him through the brightly illuminated corridors of the U.S. embassy, past an interior courtyard with a fountain, past a canteen, a travel agency for the staff. Hand-written English-language notices pinned to message boards recruited for cookie-bakes and excursions or offered last-chances. Most of the people striding from office to office were big and pale or big and black. You wouldn't have remembered you were in Colombia at all if it hadn't been for the security guards and the secretaries and other low-level employees.

"I have to say I'm very curious about this misguided young fellow."

71

The flak varied the tone of his voice when he pronounced the last three words, making fun of them. He always spoke in a self-conscious, guarded way, so you wondered whether it was just his job or whether he was like that all the time.

"He's one crazy, mixed-up kid all right."

"Yeah."

They went into a meeting room with a large table. There was a map of Colombia on one wall and on another a print of a nineteenth-century oil painting depicting mountains and a plunging waterfall somewhere in the United States. The painting, although realistic, was in a heroic style which implied that any inhabitant of that dramatic geography must share in its scale. The official Robert had asked to see, a tall, rangily-built man in his forties with blond hair swept back from his forehead, came in after a couple of minutes, apologising for being late. They shook hands and sat down. The flak said he couldn't use his tape recorder, but he was permitted to take out a notebook.

"I saw you out jogging the other day," said Robert.

"Oh yeah? I've got to be more careful," said the official.

"Bogota's not that bad."

"Hey, that's right. But you tell people who haven't been here, and they don't get it. I love this place."

"Yeah, it's not bad is it? People think it's like Kabul or something. But you can live well here. There are some good restaurants, and it's cheap."

"Uh huh. So, how can I help you?"

"So. Okay, let's start with, how interested are you guys in Comrade Martín? What do you know about him?"

The official rubbed his close-shaved throat and smiled. Then he looked at the flak.

"Background briefing, right?"

"Yes, as I explained to Robert earlier, he can only refer to an unnamed U.S. official, without mentioning the embassy or specifying the physical location. He can't say you're in Bogota."

"Okay," said the official. "You know, I'm really not so interested in him, he's just a poor screwed-up little jerk. My interest is really in the FARC, and every detail I can, uh, glean about those guys is useful for my job. So, you know, he's not a big issue, but he does tell me about their organisation. He's not a policy issue himself. He's got no political significance at all."

"Nope," said the flak.

"The United States is fully committed to support for the Colombian government, so the fact that this kid has gotten himself mixed up with a criminal organisation is really neither here nor there. There are plenty of wrong-doers in the States too, unfortunately."

"We'd probably visit him in jail, though," said the flak. "As a United States citizen we would have responsibilities to him in the event that he was caught."

The official nodded. "And, while we're not interested in him as an individual, we are interested in what he's doing as a criminal."

"So, what do you know about him? He seems to think no one knows he's there."

The official and the flak both sniggered, so Robert sniggered too.

"Oh, we know who he is. I can't say how, of course. I can say the Colombians have been in touch with us about him."

"Yes, I've been speaking to the Colombians too. They've given me a name, I wondered if you could confirm it for me."

The flak said, "I don't think so, Robert. Sorry."

"It's Jesse something, isn't it? Jesse Sorker, Sorky. Something like that?"

The official only smiled.

"Come on, give me a break. You know the Colombians always get the spelling wrong."

"Do they? No, I really can't tell you."

"Can you at least tell me where he's from?"

"No."

"He was studying, wasn't he? He was at college? Can you at least tell me where? What he was studying?"

The official smirked. "I'll tell you that. This is funny. This guy was studying accounting."

"Jesus Christ. Accounting? He was studying accounting? And now he's in the FARC. What college was he at?"

The flak interjected. "I don't think we could say anything about his identity. It would really not be appropriate. There's a criminal investigation under way, you can say that that's the reason. But it just wouldn't be convenient at just this time."

"Come on," said Robert, "don't be teases. What does it matter where he was studying? That doesn't give anything material away."

"Sorry, it just wouldn't be appropriate."

"Okay," Robert said. "So why don't you tell me what you can say about this guy."

The official's face was temporarily given over to a look of deep abstraction. He frowned and looked at the floor. He pushed one hand back through his hair, sighing. Then, successfully concluding this period of consideration, he leant forward, making a frank, illustrative gesture with open hands.

"You know," he said, "he's lost in time. He still thinks it's 1967. But the FARC aren't what they used to be. They're a narco-trafficking organisation. As to him, well, it's just a theory, but I think he's probably one of those quiet, nerdy guys who just freaks out. Plays too many computer games. Stays in his room all the time, all musty like. Just sucks in all his aggression. Then. One day. Bam! Rat-a-tat-tat! A lot of dead jocks."

Later, as they left the meeting room, the flak said, "Robert, can I ask you a favour?"

"Sure."

"I didn't want to say this when he was still there, but, that remark about what the guy studied, could you please just treat that as something you found out yourself? Please don't ascribe those remarks to the U.S. official, he really shouldn't have said that. And it doesn't really make much difference to you where you got that from, it's just a lead."

"Okay, don't worry," said Robert.

"Cool. These guys, sometimes you just never know what they're going to come out with and say."

A Marine with massive forearms kept vigil within a bullet-proof glass cabin. Robert went out through pale green bronze doors, heavy as an airlock, and crossed an empty courtyard to a fortified guard post, where he retrieved his mobile phone. Colombians who had requested visas were queuing at another entrance, by a broad, sterile lawn. Once outside the steel perimeter fence, he took an authorised taxi. Concrete barriers prevented ordinary traffic from driving by the embassy compound.

He got out near the Parque de la 93 and bought some German beer at a shop selling imported foodstuffs. Walking the few blocks to his home, the chilled cans swinging in doubled-up plastic bags, he passed the Spanish consulate, where several hundred people stood waiting in the bright sun. They wanted visas too. They wanted to escape to Europe. Some of them had probably bunked down on the beaten-up pavement overnight to make sure they had a good position in the queue. They were a scruffy bunch. Women, bulging in the wrong places, had elaborately painted nails and tattooed eyebrows, the men wore cheap, baggy denim or stiff, inappropriate suits. They were mainly black or mestizo. A female street vendor in a baseball cap, trailed by two small children, was selling sweet black coffee from a thermos flask.

Until just recently, the Spanish had used to make people wait outside their embassy, which was on the other side of the Parque de la 93, but the diplomats, tired of having to pick their way through a crowd to get to work each morning, got rid of them by opening the separate consulate, just opposite an Italian restaurant. The people wanting to emigrate to Spain scared away the Italian restaurant's more elegant clientele, and so it gave up and closed down and reopened with a blackboard offering cut-price breakfasts of rib soup and maize arepas, and charging for use of a photocopier and a telephone.

At home, Robert sat at his desk and called a features editor on a newspaper in the United States.

"Listen, I've got the story just about ready. Gringo guerrilla."

"Hey, hey, hey!" said the editor. "Hey! That's great."

"You'll never believe this. The guy used to study accounting at college in the States. And then he becomes a Marxist rebel."

"Oh, you're shitting me! Isn't it usually the other way round? That's great."

"No, they told me at your embassy this morning. It's a fabulous story."

"You know. Hey. Congratulations. I can't wait to read it. I think it's great how you go out there to these wild places. How long were you out there? Like, a week? Running risks. Not everyone is prepared to do that."

"Thanks," said Robert.

77

"Hey, can you e-mail the photos first? Like now perhaps?"

"Right. That's my problem. He didn't want to be photographed."

"No photos! Oh shit, no photos. Shit! What a jerk."

"Well, he just wouldn't let us. You can't sneak photos of these guys either. Or else their friends come and get you when they realise what you did."

"Of course, I totally understand. You're totally right. Totally. It's just, the story's not worth the same without photos."

"Not worth the same? No, I suppose not," said Robert.

He had hoped to call television producers too, but he had never got the video.

That stupid cunt, he thought, thinking of Martín with more frustration than bitterness. Or Jesse. Or whatever his name was.

He went to the kitchen and made himself a mug of tea. Then he sat down on the rented sofa with heavy wooden armrests and watched through the sliding doors as an afternoon rainstorm flash-flooded the red and blue tiles of his small patio. He still had a chance with Martín, he thought. He just had to be patient. He could still do it properly. The guy had liked him after all. And he had given him an e-mail address. Even the FARC had e-mail these days, at least occasionally. And why would he give him his address, if it wasn't because he had liked him?

❏ ❏ ❏

A man answered the phone in America. He had an aged, unsteady voice.

"Hello?"

Robert said, "Hi, good afternoon, I'm looking for Jesse Soj-ka, Soy-ka. I'm sorry, I'm not sure how to pronounce his surname."

"It's Soy-ka. It's Polish. Like soy sauce. But there's no Jesse here. Excuse me, may I ask who's calling, please?"

That was Martín's real name. Sojka. Robert had finally got it from a contact at the Colombian National Police, whom he had once taken to lunch. The man had done him a favour and copied the details from the immigration card the young American had filled in when he had entered the country as a tourist a year earlier.

Jesse Sojka. He had been born on June 15, 1976. He had boarded an American Airways flight in Chicago on his way to the revolution.

On his laptop, Robert had gone into a search engine and found "Telephone Directory Chicago". He had entered "Jesse Sojka" into the suggested field, but that didn't bring up anything. Plain "Sojka" yielded 33 entries, with names, addresses and numbers.

First on the list was Arnold Sojka, who lived at 360 W Illinois Street, Chicago, IL. But Arnold was clearly a suspicious man, querulous and quick to anger.

"Excuse me, who's calling please?"

"Is that Mr Arnold Sojka? I'm a friend of Jesse's, and I'm trying to find his family. He's got into a bit of trouble and needs some help. Would you know any Jesse Sojka?"

"Listen, who are you? What's going on? How did you get my number? I don't know no Jesse. Who the heck are you? What do you mean, Colombia?"

"I'm sorry, it's a mistake."

"Now you just hold on!"

Robert hung up.

He tried the next number, and the next. There were a lot of Poles in Chicago. He worked his way down the list.

There is a chore which journalists usually dread. On the small newspaper in rural Norfolk where Robert had obtained his first job, this was known as "the death knock". It refers to the moment when a reporter knocks on the door of the family of someone who has just been killed. To a small newspaper in an English country town, even some-one killed in a traffic accident can be a story. But, for it to be a good story, you need a reaction from the family, hence the death knock. A reporter knocks on the door and asks them how they feel. It is a pretty stupid question. But usu-ally, to Robert's permanent surprise and guilty gratitude, they answered. This could be because it was necessary for them to share their grief, it could be because it was impo-lite to refuse a response, or it could be because journalists make people feel important.

The situation he was in, Jesse Sojka was pretty close to dead.

The fifth or sixth number on Robert's list was answered by a woman.

Chemically calm, enunciating with disturbing precision, she said, "That was his father's name. Sojka. It's not my name. My name's Arroyo. I use my maiden name now. For years I've used it."

Robert switched on his speaker phone and his cassette recorder. A pneumatic drill began smashing up tarmac on the street outside, so he raised his voice as he said, "Ms Arroyo, I've seen your son."

Then there was silence. A random crackle on the fibre optics. So he said, "I'm a journalist, and I've seen him. A week ago now. We had quite a long chat. My name's Robert Hoggard. I work for ..."

And he repeated his usual list of names. His voice always droned a bit when he did that, even during a death knock moment.

"Hello? Are you still there, Ms Arroyo?"

The red light glowed on his cassette recorder but there wasn't anything to record. Just the sly sound of his own wheedling and coaxing, and the intermittent punk clamour of the pneumatic drill outside his flat, smashing up a potholed street in Bogota.

"If you want to check that I am who I say I am, just call one of the papers I mentioned."

And then, finally, after a long time, a continent's stretch distant, he heard her give up on something and sigh. Her words, when they eventually came, emerged slowly, softly, as if she was listening to herself speak before absent-mindedly tossing them into the ether.

"Listen, I care a lot about my son, I love him very deeply. I always gave him everything."

The drill had gone quiet.

Robert spoke in a paused, syrupy way.

"I'm sure, Ms Arroyo. I'm absolutely sure of that. You're his mother. He worries about you, about the effect that what he's doing might have on you."

"Where did you say you were from? You're a reporter? You're working for ... "

He repeated his list. His best, low, calm voice.

"Don't worry, I'm not from the FBI or the CIA or anything."

"No, not with that type of British accent. Very cute."

That was nearly a laugh, a sort of not-quite-flirtatious, sobbing giggle.

"I don't want to get him into trouble," she said.

"Of course not. It's not about that, Ms Arroyo."

And then he said, "I'm sorry to ring you up about this. It would be better in person, but I'm in Colombia."

"Can you tell me how he was?"

He could. This was doing her a favour, in a way. So he said, "Jesse seemed fine. You know, I was invited to meet him, by the people he's with." Robert didn't say who these people were, out of habit, in case his phone was bugged. "He was in very good shape. I brought him some chocolate. He liked that, he doesn't get that where he is, you know. He hasn't got many luxuries, but he seemed in good shape. He seemed in good spirits, Ms Arroyo."

"Chocolate? That was nice of you. Poor boy. Did he have any message for me?"

She was drawling. In fact, she sounded like she might be doped. He noted that it had not occurred to her that it might not have been her son who had revealed his real identity.

"He's worried," said Robert. "He's worried that you might get in trouble because of him."

He just wanted to make her feel comfortable so she could talk. But then she said, "He's worried? He's worried? One e-mail. One lousy e-mail in a whole fucking year. Do you think that's right? What was your name?"

"Hoggard. Robert."

"Do you think that's right, Hoggard? One e-mail?"

Robert was taken aback. He tried to calm her, to steer her back in the right direction.

"It's difficult for Jesse. I saw how he lives. He's in the jungle. And, you know, the authorities are after him. Could you tell me a bit about him? Was he always so idealistic?"

"Idealistic? Was he idealistic? No."

Abruptly, her tone had become milder, softening from anger to confusion.

"What was he then? Maybe you can tell me a bit about him, some anecdote perhaps? Did he stand up to the bullies in high school? What sort of kid was he? He must have been popular. Lots of girlfriends, I'm sure."

But Ms Arroyo yawned.

"You know," she said. "You know, this is getting to be a bit of a drag."

"I'm sorry, Ms Arroyo. I'm sorry. I know it must be hard. Maybe I can help you send a message to your son. Is he your only child?"

"It's just that you're asking all these," she groped for the word with the same puzzled languor, before concluding, with unbalanced venom, "*questions!*"

"I'm sorry. I'm really sorry about that. Listen, are you feeling okay?"

"I'm okay. Thank you for asking."

"You're welcome. You know, I'd ask if there was anything I could do, but, you know, I'm in a different country."

She said, "That's sweet. You're nice, Mr … Mr whatever your name was. Mr Journalist."

"That's okay, Ms Arroyo. May I ask your first name?"

"Yes, of course you may. It's Janice."

Robert said, "Janice. It sounds like you've had a rough time."

"It's tough. Tough for a girl. You know, I'm on my own now, so things aren't so much fun."

She laughed. A dry, scratchy sound, like shaking a packet of cigarettes.

"Look, Janice, would you happen to have any photographs of your son you could lend me? From his student days, perhaps? A snapshot?"

"I've got snapshots. If you want to see them."

"You do? I can organise to have someone go and get them. I have your address."

Then she was confused again.

84

"Of me, too, if you want to see them," she said.

"Oh, that would be nice. That would be very nice, Janice. And look, Janice, can I ask you a simple, straightforward question?"

But something had gone wrong.

"No. You know what, Hoggard?" she said. "No, you can't ask a question. You know what you can do? Go fuck yourself! That's what you can do."

Eight

The day he was due to meet Milena at the airport, he realised he didn't want to pick her up in some old yellow cab, and so he rented a big Mitsubishi four-wheel drive. Usually he was very careful about money, but the cost of the car didn't add much to what he was already paying for her plane ticket and hotel. A city is a very different place when you have a car than it is when you are used to relying on your feet; it's smaller and more exclusive. You feel more a part of the economy.

The sky was blue when they dropped off the four-wheel drive outside his block of flats. He hadn't driven regularly for several years, but the Mitsubishi was an automatic and easy to manage even though he wasn't used to being so high above the road. For a while, he coasted through tree-lined, quiet streets near where he lived and that was easy except for potholes. But then he got trapped on a major arterial road which was clogged with buses pulling over to pick up passengers without warning or veering into following traffic. A beggar tapped at his electric window when he stopped at a traffic light. Sitting in the high cabin, listening to the stereo, Robert felt he could be anywhere in the world where you could spend money on technology. But the beggar was definitely in Bogota.

Somehow he managed to get up above the city, and followed a straining truck up a steep curving road into La Calera. He crossed over the hump of a mountain and drove for a while through bumpy green meadows and patches of eucalyptus. Then the sky clouded over, it began to drizzle, and he drove back to his apartment to wait.

He drank just one beer and watched football on TV, lying on his bed. He couldn't concentrate on work. He tried to picture Milena's face. But the more he thought about her, the less he was able to remember exactly what she looked like, and, finally, she just wasn't there any more. That was the way the brain worked, it was like trying to snatch a handful of smoke.

Maybe she wouldn't show up anyway, he thought. And then, so what? He didn't know her anyway. So, if she didn't come, he wouldn't lose anything. Just some money. And then he thought, and what if she does come, and things go badly. Then she'll just go home, he thought. I'll make her do that.

Then there was the question of what she saw in him.

He got up and went to the bathroom and looked at his face in the mirror. His face was more or less the same as ever. Then he pulled up his shirt and looked at his belly.

If things go badly, she'll just go home, he thought. And if she doesn't show up, it doesn't matter.

At the airport, he stood outside the domestic arrivals exit, car keys in his pocket. The arrivals hall was closed off by sliding doors, coated with a chipped mirror, and he looked inside towards the baggage belts each time they opened to see if Milena was there. When the doors closed again he was left inspecting his own reflection in their scratched surface.

It doesn't matter, he thought. Whatever happens, whatever she is, it doesn't matter.

Arriving passengers emerged in a hurry. The poorer they looked, the more luggage they were likely to be carrying, the greater the suspicion that they had left nothing behind they couldn't cram into the aeroplane's cabin. Some lugged vinyl suitcases and clothes stuffed in plastic bags, others had loaded trolleys with cardboard boxes, bulging and secured from bursting by masking tape, packed with tatty, precious belongings, with browning avocados or fig fudge or cracked crockery.

Then he saw her. She was carrying an old denim bag and frowning as she left the airport building, looking for him.

"Milena." He liked saying her name.

She was just as he had remembered her. And he didn't feel ashamed of her either.

She gave him her pouting little girl's smile.

"I was afraid you wouldn't be here."

"You were afraid?"

"I thought maybe you'd decide you didn't want to see me after all, and you just wouldn't come and I'd arrive and I'd be on my own in Bogota, with nowhere to go and no money."

"How could you think that, Milena?"

They kissed on the cheeks. Just the standard Latin greeting. He took her bag and they walked towards where he had left the four-wheel drive, past all the people who looked at the big awkward gringo and the beautiful young girl, through the untidy car park with its eucalyptus trees under the grey sky.

"It's cold," she said.

He laughed. This gave him something to say.

"No, it's not. Colombians always say Bogota's cold, but it's not really. You should try Europe in winter, with snow."

She shivered at the very suggestion. She was wearing a denim jacket and jeans, with platform shoes, which made her walk with a slight inclination, as if she was skating in slow motion. Her hair was now red and she was perfectly made up, which he took as a compliment.

"I thought you might decide you didn't want to see me. And then what would I have done? All alone here without knowing anyone."

He looked at her, and then he thought of what he looked like himself.

"Nice car," she said, when they got to the four-wheel drive, which bleeped and clicked when he pressed the button on the key ring to unlock the doors. An expensive car is an impressive thing, he thought. It's like seeing a better life you can just climb into and drive off in.

"Thanks. It's not mine, I've just got it for a few days." Then he added, "I'm getting another one." And, although he had never thought about buying a car until that moment, he meant it.

He put her bag in the back seat. It clinked, with make-up tubs or lipstick tubes or some such. Then they got in.

"You didn't bring a lot with you, for a woman," he said, and immediately feared he might have offended her. Because she might not have much to bring.

"I don't need much," she said, and smiled, settling into her seat and raising her chin.

She had two very different attitudes with which to confront the world. They were immediately recognizable: the first was that little girl look, an appeal for male protection; the other was a haughty display of beauty, defiant and unsentimental but also calculated for its impact on men.

"I'm so glad you came," he repeated, and then he praised her appearance. He was aware of a problem of tone in their conversation. But they both knew why he had invited her. She acknowledged the compliment with a smile.

"Do you think so?"

He did, so he repeated what he had said, and then added, "Your town is a poorer place without you today."

"Huh. It's a pretty poor place when I'm there too."

Her beauty was a safe subject. It was the main thing he knew about her.

"We're going to have a great time," said Robert, and this was a happy formula, suggesting as it did an equality of aims between them.

He turned the key in the ignition and the stereo came on too loud, so he switched it off.

"No, put it back on. I like to listen to music," said Milena.

"I'll take you to your hotel, so you can freshen up and leave your things."

"Okay."

He pulled out of the car park and felt good about the four-wheel drive. She sat with her back straight, smiling a mild, polite smile, and showing her teeth when he glanced away from the road ahead and grinned at her. Once, she lightly touched his hand above the automatic shift. Her perfume mixed with the new-car smell. He admired her profile, and imagined what the two of them must look like to people on the street as they passed.

"So, how does Bogota seem?" he said, as they progressed down a highway lined by square office buildings beyond the grassy verges. A soldier with an assault rifle stood vigil overhead on a steel pedestrian bridge and a wavy line of dark mountains terminated the horizon.

"Big," she replied, accurately.

"Too big?"

"No, it's good it's big. My town is too small. Everyone knows you. People criticise you, everyone's always spying on you and talking behind your back."

"That town's full of paramilitaries," he said.

"Yes, but it's not just them."

She looked out the window.

"Who could possibly speak badly of you?"

She snorted, but it was a pretty sound, a high-pitched humph.

"Women," she said.

91

Initially, he had thought he would book her a room in a small, very smart hotel converted from an old colonial house. But he had guessed that she would be more impressed by a thoroughly modern place. He pulled up by the Sofitel, where a man with a mirror on a pole and golden retriever dog checked the car for bombs and a valet drove it off to a subterranean bay.

Robert noticed that the receptionist glared at Milena before preparing her key card.

"What's this?" she asked, as they turned away.

"That's the key. There's a slot in the door," said Robert.

"Thank you," she said, "Could you wait for me?"

Robert was disappointed she hadn't invited him up to her room, but said nothing. He waited in an armchair in the lobby, looking at the marble and brass as a French airline crew arrived, wheeling neat black suitcases and laughing. You didn't see many foreigners in Bogota, so he noticed them. When Milena returned, some time later, she had changed into a mini skirt and high heels, and they went outside. It was 6.45 and the sky was a deepening indigo. There were soot-black clouds. He led her on the short walk to the restaurant where he had thought they would have dinner. It was early but this was the next thing they had to do. A one-legged teenage beggar whined at Robert for money and he gave him a few coins.

There were just a couple of bored bodyguards gossiping outside the restaurant, which was on a corner across from the Centro Andino shopping centre on a short T-shaped pedestrian strip lined with places to drink and eat. The manager shook Robert's hand and smiled at Milena in a nice way meant as a compliment to both of them. Robert felt proud of her, but also relieved that no one would be likely to recognise her here in Bogota.

They sat in the middle of the restaurant, surrounded by other tables yet to be filled, and Robert ordered a glass of white wine and Milena a fresh mandarin juice. The place was spacious with bare brick walls, only very faintly lit, and was very popular with Bogota's rich. It advertised its food as Belgian, and had a seafood bar with oysters on ice. The menu was in French, so Milena couldn't understand it.

"That's duck," said Robert.

"Ugh, no," she said.

"Rabbit. Mussels."

"Ugh. What are mussels?"

"Shellfish. They look a bit like old women's genitals."

"That's disgusting. Don't be rude."

He liked this early suggestion of ownership.

"I'm sorry. It's my sense of humour. I'm always making jokes. I suppose I'm kind of nihilistic. I never know whether anything's important so I just make jokes about everything."

"What's nihilistic?"

"It's what I've just said, when you don't believe in anything."

"You don't believe in anything?"

"Of course I do," he said.

"Then why do you make jokes?"

"Don't you ever make jokes?"

"Yes," she said. And then she added, "Families are important."

"You're right there. Tell me about yours."

The waiter interrupted them to take their order. Milena asked for an entrée followed by a steak. She asked if she could order dessert too, but the waiter apologised and told her that she could ask for it after the main course.

Robert ordered duck, and Milena said, "How can you eat a duck? The poor thing."

"What about cows? Why do you feel sorry for ducks and not cows?"

"Ducks are so cute."

"Cows are cute too. And they're more intelligent than ducks."

"How do you know?"

"They've got bigger brains," said Robert.

"You should eat mussels then, if it's about brains."

"I prefer duck. It's delicious, very fatty, like a flying pig."

It turned out that she liked to talk and he was happy for her to take over the conversation. She spoke mainly about her family. About her late father, her struggling mother, her unfortunate sisters.

Then she repeated that she had been afraid that he would not show up at the airport. That would have been ridiculous, he thought, after persuading her to come and then buying her a ticket, but he didn't quite say it like that. He had persuaded her to drink some red wine, and he could see how her cheeks were slightly flushed beneath her make up. Her cosmetics made her appear more vulnerable, he thought, and then he imagined how she would have looked at the airport if he really hadn't turned up.

He told her he had a daughter and then wondered whether it would have been better not to mention it.

"How lovely she must be," she said.

He explained that he didn't see her often, only once or twice a year, and that even that was difficult to manage.

"Poor little girl. She must miss her papa," said Milena, and then she looked him in the eyes, "Why don't you go back and stay with her?"

"Because of her mother," said Robert.

Milena smiled.

"But if she's the mother of your daughter, you must want to be with her too."

"No," said Robert.

"Poor little girl. I know what it's like not to have a father."

Robert didn't like her tone.

"It must have been very tough for you," he said.

Then Milena started talking about how the guerrillas had killed her father, and it was strange but Robert noticed how this was obviously an easier subject for her and he saw how it relaxed her.

"I hate them, the guerrillas," she said. "You know they took the ransom money, everything my mother could get together, and then they killed him anyway. They told her they would sell her the body if she liked. Can you imagine what that was like? She had no money, no husband, and three small daughters. It amazes me she didn't go mad. I would have gone mad."

She was happy again, leaning towards him and looking beautiful.

"This country's all mixed up," he said. But violence wasn't such an interesting subject.

"This country's wonderful but it's shit too," she said. And then she added, "Money's all that counts. Not a human being, not a father, not his children. They should kill them all. I hope they kill them all."

"Kill who?" asked Robert. He had been looking at her and wondering about her.

"The guerrillas," she said.

The waiter arrived to ask about dessert. Milena had finished her steak. She had a good appetite. Robert had eaten well too, and drunk most of the bottle of red wine.

"Do you think I'm old?" he asked, after she had ordered a chocolate soufflé.

She laughed and took his hand across the table.

"Old? I think you're perfect, a very good age. You know, I don't like boys."

He had already forgotten that they had just been talking about her father, and pointed out that she was young enough to be his daughter. But it didn't seem to matter to her either.

"You're a perfect age. You're a man," she repeated.

"I don't want to speak to you any more. I just want to watch you," he said.

She smiled. Robert sat back and looked around the restaurant, which had filled up now. He couldn't see any woman nearly as good-looking as Milena. Her company made him feel more at home in Bogota.

"You are making me nervous," she said, and he liked that idea.

"Say something," she said.

"Why? You're beautiful. I've already said it. Why say it again? They're just words."

"I like words. Say something pretty to me."

"Dessert," he said. "That's a pretty word." And the waiter served the soufflé.

"Say something else."

"Okay. When I look at you I want to protect you," he said.

After dinner, which he paid for with cash, they went out onto the street and he took her hand again.

"You know, Robert," she said, "we're still getting to know each other."

"And we are getting to know each other," he said, putting his arm around her shoulders. She slipped out easily from beneath his bicep.

"You're an English gentleman, remember," she said.

"Yeah."

An old man in a striped suit began hopping along beside them and read Milena a line of bad poetry, so Robert gave him 500 pesos. Then he bought a single rose in a clear plastic tube from a woman who had bound her sleeping baby to her belly with a blanket, and presented it to Milena, who held it before her and looked at it as they walked.

"Would you like to go somewhere else? To dance, maybe?"

He didn't know anywhere at all for dancing, just many places which were good for drinking, but they went to a bar with a huge picture of a grinning crocodile. The place was packed and people were dancing on wooden tables. Milena danced well but Robert was self-conscious.

"You drank a lot," she said, leaning towards him and shouting above the music.

She stopped dancing. Then he tried to give her a kiss, but she shied away from him, averting her eyes, as if she had just seen something on the other side of the bar and had moved suddenly to get a better look.

He tried three times and each time she dodged him like a boxer.

"Let's go," she said, and took his hand.

Outside, quickly, she gave him a sudden kiss on a cheek. Her reflexes were just much faster than his.

"You've been so nice," she said.

They walked along the dark street. There were several beggars. A little further along after the hotel was the huge, walled mansion of a dead drug lord. It had been confiscated by the authorities but they hadn't been able to sell it because potential buyers were afraid of reprisals.

They stopped in front of the hotel and Robert looked at

Milena and smiled and wondered how best to suggest that he go up to her room.

Then she said, "Good night, Robert. What time shall I see you tomorrow?"

He didn't know what to say. He turned red in the dark.

"I'll come round," he said. "I'll give you a call."

In the morning, Robert collected Milena and took her to three different shopping malls. One before lunch and two afterwards. He had asked her what she had wanted to do. She would go into boutiques and pick things up and look at them in such a way that he would offer to buy them for her. But she only accepted one item, a pair of shoes with cork platform heels, and declined to receive anything else.

Each time he took out his wallet she said *Qué pena*. This means "what a pity" and is an expression Colombians use to excuse themselves when they bump into you in the street.

She window-shopped and he took some pleasure by observing how people looked at him with her. Despite her beauty, he felt less conspicuous with her than he did when he was alone in these places. Her presence made it obvious why he was there. People need other people that way. Their wants lend purpose, they moor you to the world. The shopping centres were full of families in new clothes strolling past the window displays.

"*Qué pena*," said Milena, after asking for another mandarin juice in the restaurant at lunchtime.

"You don't have to say that."

"It's just you're paying for everything. You know I'd pay if I could."

Robert was drinking a second glass of white wine.

"Don't be silly, I invited you to come," he said. "And it doesn't matter to me."

The restaurant faced a little square with some trees and a white church, and Milena said, "I always wanted a house in the mountains, with big windows, so you can see the sky, and watch when it rains."

Robert had begun to feel like a fool. He wasn't going to settle for being her eunuch shopping companion and thought that he would like to say something to hurt her.

"Why did you accept my invitation?" he asked.

"What a question. Why? I like you, that's why."

"But you didn't know who I was. We only spoke for a couple of hours. I could be a psychopath, some mad murderer, for all you knew."

"You're not a psychopath," she said, and he laughed.

The sky had clouded over by the time they finished lunch and left the restaurant. It began to drizzle as they walked down a cobbled street.

"I like walking in the rain," said Milena. Then it began to fall harder, and they rushed to the waiting four-wheel drive. They slammed the doors shut, but Robert had to open his again when the cripple who had been looking after the car came over for his tip.

The rain drummed on the car's roof and streamed down the windscreen. Robert hadn't finished yet.

"I haven't asked you about men, your old boyfriends."

"Don't. They don't matter. And there's no one."

"But, a girl like you ..." he said.

Then he dropped it.

He turned the key in the ignition switch and the CD player came on. He drove off through the rain, straight into a traffic jam. The Séptima highway, which followed the contours of the lower mountains, had become a shallow, fast-flowing river. Cars advanced slowly, sending waves slapping over the kerbs. A few soaked soldiers wearing green waterproof cloaks tried to direct the line of vehicles past an army base. Drivers slammed on their steering wheels with their palms and sounded their horns to no purpose.

Milena started talking about her family again, and it was intriguing. It was like listening to a proper story. Everything was clearly such a battle that the people she described took sorry, struggling form in Robert's mind in between the sound of the rain and the windscreen wipers.

They drove into the entrance to the underground parking at the Centro Andino shopping mall and opened the back section of the car for the sniffer dog. The guards, rifles slung over their shoulders, smiled and waved them on into the parking bays.

Then they drifted through the shops. Robert's post-lunch shopping was alcohol-assisted, an easy stroll, and Milena considered the displays with the dignity of someone who is good-looking enough to know that any of the clothes for sale would suit her.

"It's not that I want to buy everything, you mustn't think that," she assured Robert. "It's just that it's so interesting. In my town they just don't have these things."

After the Centro Andino they went to the Centro Atlantis. They stood on an escalator beneath the high glass atrium and Milena looked smiling at a kids' show on an opposite deck, where a band was dressed up as cartoon animals. The atrium and other windows exposed the four stories of shops to natural light, to Bogota's aquarium grey. Most of the outlets sold women's clothes, but there was also a yellow and red Tower Records, a Kenneth Cole, a place selling Tommy Hilfiger, and a multiplex cinema. It had the international airport feel of any shopping centre anywhere, but it was quite exclusive and the guards would not have let most of the population in. Milena liked it.

By now she had allowed him to take her hand. Her plane was due to leave before lunch on Sunday.

He felt angry again, and already defeated. But he tried anyway.

"Maybe we could go back to your hotel room," he said.

They had left the Centro Atlantis, and were picking their way past the hippy street vendors selling bangles and braces and leather bags all spread out on the pavement.

She put her arms around his neck and kissed him.

"No," she said. "It's too soon."

"You're leaving tomorrow."

102

"I know, but it's still too soon," she said, and then, smiling, tugging the front of his shirt, "What sort of girl do you think I am? And I promised my mother I'd behave."

"Your mother," he said.

She nodded and let go of his hand. He tried to take it again but she wouldn't let him, fixing her eyes straight ahead in the street.

"I'm sorry," he said, and put his arm around her as they walked.

"What sort of girl do you think I am?" she repeated, but she let him keep his arm on her shoulders.

And then he had to say things to make it better. He struggled for the words. It was difficult to find things to say which were true. She was good-looking, definitely – that was why she was there – but he couldn't say just that. And what else did he know about her? He chose soft, generic words, words to fill in the blanks, hollow categories, meant for almost anyone.

She squeezed his waist, and then, without thinking about it, he said, "Tomorrow. Don't go. Stay."

Nine

The truth is that Robert often wasn't genuinely interested in the stories he wrote as journalism, but his job had become a habit. Reporting trips especially were like an anaesthetic and he needed them. Only a week after Milena moved in with him, the FARC's peace talks with the government came close to breaking down and he had to take a plane for Florencia, where he met Pacho and together they took a taxi for the demilitarised zone

He hadn't been glad to leave Milena behind, or at least he wasn't sure of being glad. But, when he climbed into the hot interior of the battered yellow Hyundai for the drive to San Vicente, he slumped into his seat and rested his head by the window in a sweet intimation of non-existence.

The taxi shook constantly on the uneven road, and the driver went at speed because it was a dangerous stretch of country and it was best to get through it as quickly as possible. The road curved through pleasant green hills, where different types of palm trees grew in clusters and they saw grazing Zebu cattle with hump backs and sagging ears and, at one point, three vultures perched in a row on a wire fence.

About an hour after they had left Florencia, the driver

slowed down, and they passed a pool of blood that had congealed on the road. Then he accelerated, putting his foot to the floor.

"That was where they killed them, right there, see," he said.

He was scared but he couldn't help smiling when he talked. His name was Geri. He was a big man, always in need of a shave, with heavy forearms and an overhanging belly. He stank and his handshake was slimy with sweat.

"They made them get out of the car and then they killed them and burnt the cab. Three of us drivers they've killed in the last three months."

"Who did it?" asked Pacho.

"Nobody knows," said Geri, with his dead man's smile.

Robert asked, "How many of you taxi drivers are there in Florencia?"

"I know exactly how many. A hundred and two."

During the first section of the two-hour drive, Geri had chatted happily and obscenely with Pacho and had been obsequious towards Robert, who was paying him almost a hundred dollars. But he wanted to get the trip done quickly, so he could get back to Florencia before nightfall. No one travelled those roads after dark, and if they arrived late in San Vicente he would have to spend the night. But that wouldn't be a good idea, because the guerrillas might think he was with the paramilitaries. And, if he had stayed the night in San Vicente, the paramilitaries might think he was a guerrilla when he made it back to Florencia. That's why

Robert had to pay him almost a hundred dollars and he went in a hurry.

The taxi had engine trouble in one of the towns of no-man's land and they coasted to a halt. Black graffiti on the walls of the houses decreed death to the guerrillas. Geri looked very worried, but another taxi driver lent him a car and Robert and Pacho switched their bags and equipment. Then the other man, thin-faced, with sucked-in cheeks, made a shaky sign of the cross over Geri before he got into the driving seat, which bounced with his weight.

"That was lucky," he said, with his silly, scared smirk.

He drove as fast as he could, with his mouth open all the time, and played chicken with oncoming trucks, only pulling away at the absolute last minute. Distracted by so much violence, the possibility of death by traffic accident didn't seem to have occurred to him.

They were waved down at an army checkpoint just before the bridge which crossed the river into FARC territory, and made to get out of the car to be frisked. Soldiers asked for their IDs and then opened the boot to search their bags, examining Pacho's cameras. A line of armoured personnel carriers and light tanks was parked on the government side of the river. The few dozen soldiers looked either murderous or half asleep. Some cleaned their assault rifles or ate soup from mess cans. One stood holding a heavy machine gun, an ammunition belt slung over his narrow shoulders and crossing his chest, so he looked like an old Mexican bandit. The privates manning the checkpoint seemed to want to harass them but couldn't think of many questions and had to let them pass.

One of them, eighteen or nineteen years old, yelled at them as they drove away. "Tell those sons of bitches we're going to kill them all."

"Okay," said Pacho.

They crossed the long bridge across the broad, dun-coloured river. The country was exactly the same, more cattle-chewed fields, gashes of orange-yellow sand, jungle with its liquid shade. But they soon began to see the marks of rebel authority: small metal signs nailed to trees and fence posts, unintentionally funny injunctions to good behaviour stamped with the initials FARC-EP.

Don't mistreat children.

Be kind to animals.

Don't cut down trees.

"Those hypocrites," said Robert, and Pacho twisted round from the front seat and grinned.

Geri turned up the radio. The guerrillas had installed their own radio station in San Vicente and travellers were well-advised to tune in. The station played Vallenatos and the FARC's own revolutionary compositions, and one such drone was playing when three guerrillas with Kalashnikovs strolled into the middle of the road and signalled for them to stop. The rebels were pretty relaxed. This was their territory now, after all. They just stood there with their guns slung on their backs, tongue-tied as usual. The least skinny of the three was a girl with chipped nail polish and a black ponytail swinging beneath her FARC beret.

"*Buenos días*," said Robert, and the guerrillas muttered their response.

"They're journalists," said Geri, indicating Robert and Pacho. He smiled and rubbed his hands, leaning back against his car so his stomach bulged. One of the rebels made a mumbled request for identity papers. He was fingering the tassled sheath of a long knife which hung at his waist. He was very shy. Violence for these people was often just an accident, thought Robert. It wasn't anything personal. He had his official Colombian identity card and press credentials with him but instead handed over the ID issued by an expensive gym in Bogota. He never went to the gym and the card had expired several months earlier. The guerrilla looked at his photo.

"Anything wrong with it?" asked Robert.

The rebel was going to give him the card back but then stopped and looked at it again. He was going to turn to his comrades to ask them something but then didn't do that either.

"There's me. That's my photo," said Robert, and the guerrilla gave him his card back and they drove off.

Now they'd passed the guerrilla sentries there wasn't anything to worry about. Occasionally they saw more rebels on the road, or filing in and out of fields or jungle. About a third of them were female. Most of them were very young, even younger than the soldiers on the other side of the river. They wore uniforms with red, yellow and blue armbands and rubber boots. On various occasions, Robert had been taken by the army to inspect FARC corpses, lined up as trophies after a successful battle, and you could tell they were guerrillas because of the boots.

The Hotel Alkalá functioned on several floors above a shop, and stood next to an extremely economical brothel. Robert knew the Alkalá well, although opinion among journalists was divided as to whether it was the best hotel in San Vicente. Rooms were expensive, at about fifteen dollars a night, but were clean and there were telephone lines. These windowless cells were painted purple and had metal doors. They were provided with a television and an electric fan but had no air-conditioning, and the showers ran with only cold water. Each room was also equipped with a mini bar stocked with beer and rum, and the hotel management left a small basket by each bed with toothpaste, a disposable razor and a packet of condoms, which had to be paid for if used.

Robert jogged up the narrow tiled staircase leading from the street to the front desk, which was attended by a sloe-eyed mestizo girl. The last time he had lodged there, Robert had made an unsuccessful pass at her when she had come to check something in his room. It had not cooled the insinuating warmth of her welcome this time round, although he was lucky to find a couple of beds still free. The Alkalá always filled up with foreign media every time there was trouble with the peace talks. Robert knew almost everyone there. A couple of agency photographers, long-haired Chileans, were lying on sofas near the reception desk, watching television and waiting for the midday news. One was boyish-looking but the other just dressed that way. A tall guy from CNN en Español had arrived with his gangling cameraman and blocked the gloomy hallway with metal equipment cases. Because almost everyone knew almost everyone else, the journalists didn't bother to lock the doors to their rooms and left laptops, expensive cameras and satphones lying all over the place. Cables had trailed through a litter of rum bottles and drink cans and dirty ashtrays.

The girl from reception posed and simpered and then Robert greeted the Chileans.

"Hey. What's going on?" he said.

"Nothing. It's as dead as fuck. Maybe tomorrow."

"Good," said Robert, whose head was throbbing from the heat and the two-hour drive. He was already feeling the hopeless boredom of the place.

"Have yourself a beer," said one of the Chileans.

He went out onto the narrow balcony with a can of cold lager and looked at the filthy, bright colours of the street. There was a sweet-and-sour odour, the smells of dust and putrefaction ineffectively screened by cologne. Mexican ranchera music blared from the adjacent brothel, townsfolk were shouting, and puny motorbikes whined and spluttered. A snuffling pig was tethered below by the entrance.

A gruff, droll voice said, "Congratulations, asshole."

"I beg your pardon?"

THE GHOST OF CHE GUEVARA

It was Klitsch. There was something nasty about Klitsch. Or more than something nasty. His malevolence was so open and frank it was just about disarming. He revealed it without hesitation, as if in expectation of connivance with what he clearly believed was a shared human frailty.

But it was okay to be rude to Klitsch, he seemed to expect it.

"What's up with you?" asked Robert.

Klitsch was leaning against the balcony, a can of Pepsi wrapped in a paper napkin in one hand. He had long, grey hair and his Hawaiian shirt hung unbuttoned from the sun-burnt triangle of his chicken-skinned throat to the shiny pouch of his swollen belly.

The man gave a squeaky, low-comic giggle.

"Hey, just hold on for a minute before you go jumping to offensive conclusions," he said, "What a story. Congratulations."

"Thanks. So, what are you talking about?"

"The story on that bonehead who joined the FARC. So, for a third time, congratulations. And boy, did you ever fuck him over. But, hey, we're all assholes in this game."

Klitsch smiled. His teeth were large and straight, but stained. His face looked as if it had been sandpapered. Only the very blue eyes provided a clue to the one-time existence of a younger, more innocent Klitsch.

"I didn't fuck him over. I just reported what he said," said Robert.

"In this case, same thing. Wow."

The pig snuffled loudly and an unseen man swore on the street below.

Robert said, "Listen, he agreed to speak to me. The thing is, if you've got the contacts you get the story. If you don't, you don't."

Klitsch, who was in fact oddly free of professional envy, put on a hurt face.

"Oh, but I did say it was a great story, didn't I? I said congratulations, didn't I?"

"Well, thanks. But I didn't fuck him over."

Robert wanted to walk away. But he stayed where he was. Maybe he deserved his punishment.

"Now hold on," said Klitsch raising a hand in the air. "Yes you did fuck him over. But I've done the same. We all do that. We're journalists after all, aren't we? That's what we do, use and abuse. We betray people. Love them and leave them. Wham, bam, thank you Ma'am."

Robert took a drink of his lager. What really annoyed him about Klitsch was the way he clearly enjoyed suggesting they were on the same moral level.

"Look, if anyone fucked that guy over it was him, by getting himself into that situation in the first place. All I did was describe it," he said.

"And sold the story," said Klitsch, "It's like gossip really, or pornography, a pornography of pain. It has no other justification sometimes, and we don't really know why it has to be that way, but it does. We just don't know anything different."

He had an ugly, throaty voice. His accent was, Robert

judged, from New York or New Jersey or thereabouts.

"It's not pornography," said Robert.

"Oh yes it is. And you know it is too. And, I repeat, it was a good story," continued Klitsch. "I also liked the quotes from the mother."

"You're a weird guy, Jacob," said Robert, finishing his beer. He crushed the can.

The American smiled, showing off his surprisingly straight teeth.

"I prefer it when you call me, Klitsch, Robert."

When the peace process had begun, Robert had ill-advisedly written a story for a U.S. newspaper about the extraordinary number of brothels in San Vicente. They mainly catered to coca growers and were sad-looking places with short flapping curtains facing the street instead of front doors, so you could see the shiny legs of the girls in miniskirts sitting at wooden tables waiting for customers. Robert had visited several of these cantinas with Pacho, buying a drink in each and trying to strike up a conversation with the prostitutes, girls from small villages who were very concerned their families wouldn't find out what they were doing. By coincidence, Klitsch had often worked for the same newspaper, and, when Robert had mentioned its name, more than one of the girls said, ah, like our friend Klits. They also mentioned guerrilla customers and the story offended the FARC. It took him months to repair relations.

"Gotta go," said Robert.

"But it's lunchtime. And there's nothing going on today.

Sweet nothing at all. Why don't we go get something to eat?"

"Just got to do something," said Robert, and he left Klitsch alone on the balcony.

Pacho was in his room watching television.

"Let's go to lunch," said Robert. "We can drop by the FARC office first."

The FARC had set up what it called a public relations office on the dusty main square. The female guerrilla in charge didn't trust reporters and seldom told them anything. She wasn't there anyway. A tall, vanilla-ice-cream-blond American freelance photographer who Robert knew arrived just after he did.

"Nora's not there?" he asked.

"What do you think?" smiled Robert.

"Aw, shit. She told me she was going to get here half an hour ago."

"She's a waste of time anyway."

"Yeah. Hey, where'd you get those boots?"

"Buenos Aires."

"Oh, damn. They're killer boots."

The three of them went to lunch in the Toro Negro just a few doors away. This was a large concrete shed which the owners of the Alkalá had converted into a restaurant to take advantage of the presence of the journalists and officials attending the peace talks. Two long tables were already full of reporters, mainly foreigners. The most edible parts of the menu were grilled chicken or steak or fried cachama, a river fish which arrived with everything except most of the

114

guts and tasted like mud with needles. As was the case with the Alkalá, the Toro Negro was the best establishment in town. Its principal attractions were approximate hygiene, the availability of chilled beer, and the advantage that when you were inside you weren't out in the sun.

The reporters had finished watching their Colombian colleagues on the midday news and were discussing whether the talks would collapse.

"What's your angle?" one asked another.

"Fear. The usual. The locals all think the paramilitaries will come and chop them up with chainsaws if the talks fold."

"Yeah, that's what I did too. I did it last year as well but it's the only way into it."

"And they're right to be scared," said a blond woman with a sun-dried complexion, "Everyone here's been doing business with the guerrillas – they've got no choice – so the paramilitaries would kill them, or at least a whole lot of them."

"Poor old Yasmín," said one of the reporters. That was the name of the receptionist at the Alkalá.

"And you know what?" said the woman. "We won't be here to cover it if they do start killing them. San Vicente won't be a story any more. Just like it never was in the past."

"We should come back to see what happens. Don't you think we kind of owe it to them?"

"Yeah, but how many of us will?" said the woman.

"They're doing good business in the meantime. Look at all of us here, spending."

"It's kind of weird, isn't it? I mean, they're making money out of us reporting on events which could lead to their deaths."

All in all, it was an unusually ethical conversation for a group of reporters. But the yellow-haired American wasn't listening. He was commenting on the food to a group of fellow photographers.

"Yucca. Fuck, man. I just love this yucca. When I can't get a good old piece of wood for my midday meal, I opt for yucca."

Another photographer, a big man with long hair, replied in a soft voice, "Oh, don't complain. Just nudge it to one side of your plate like a good boy, and eat the rice, potato and beans instead. And that corn. And you could ask for some bread, too."

"It's just so fibrous. It's like a bundle of twigs all glued together with gunk."

"Maybe they've got pasta too. Excuse me! Miss! *Señorita!*"

"No way, man. I prefer my carbs to come from beer, thank you very much."

Robert was sitting next to the very serious and supernaturally neat correspondent of the *New York Times*, who was the single living creature in San Vicente not coated in sweat.

"You going up to Los Pozos?" the *Times* man asked, sipping bottled water.

"I don't know. What's the point anyway, until tomorrow? It's a hell of a drive."

"Probably no point. But I'll probably go anyway, to see if any of the negotiators are around."

Such zeal, typical of the *Times* man, made Robert feel guilty.

"Maybe we can share a cab?" he said.

"Okay."

Robert chewed quickly, trying to swallow his food before he had time to dwell on the conditions in which it had been prepared. Made thirsty by heat and conviviality, he drank four beers.

He excused himself to the *Times* correspondent.

"I'm just going for a walk. I'll see you, in ..."

"One hour, at the Alkalá. Is that okay? I have to speak to an editor."

Pacho was sitting at the Spanish-speaking end of the table, talking to the Chileans. Robert slapped him on the back and told him he was going to Los Pozos. Pacho said there was nothing to photograph there until tomorrow so he might as well stay.

Klitsch came in just as Robert was settling his bill.

"Hey, leaving already?"

"Yeah, gotta run."

"Maybe I'll see you at dinner."

"Yeah, probably."

San Vicente was in its lunchtime lull. The square was empty except for a group of schoolgirls in white cotton uniforms standing in the shade of a tree. They watched Robert as he walked towards the big concrete church, the largest building in town and the only place which was always cool. There was no one there. He looked inside at a plaster Virgin and a wooden crucified Christ at the end of a line of vacant pews, but did not go in. The place smelt of detergent; it had the alkaline scent of oblivion.

A couple of guerrillas had been doing their shopping, and passed on a motorbike. They were laughing and the one who rode pillion was holding on to a haunch of beef. The sky was a blank, mineral blue. The heat smudged everything so it felt dirty. But, even at that deadest time of day, the main street had a twitching kind of automatic life. A fuzzy noise of music blew from loud speakers hung in trees round another square – the sound of a fiesta that would refuse to stop until the rebels blew up the final power pylon and the last few batteries ran out. Only some shops had their shutters drawn for business. Goods were piled on the damp concrete floors. Feather dusters and plastic buckets were suspended from their ceilings by fishing lines, their primary colours gradually becoming duller. On one side of the square there was a line of taxis waiting for any journalist who wanted to pay eighty dollars for a round trip to Los Pozos. Some of the drivers were dozing in their vehicles. Other cars were empty. As usual, there were a few kids running around, siesta-time mutineers, as prettily dressed up as their parents could afford with the money they earned from journalists or guerrillas or coca growers or government peace negotiators.

A group of rebels was seated at the rickety tables of a fly-blown bakery, drinking soft drinks. They were sitting slightly edgewise on their chairs, so they didn't have to unsling their weapons. One of them pushed long-nailed fingers back through his shiny black hair.

"Hey Hugo," said Robert.

The guerrilla sat stiff-backed, raising his chin so his narrow neck looked scrawnier. He was flattered by the attention but wanted to look superior. He didn't say anything, just looked at Robert with that amphibian, self-satisfied look. Robert didn't like the guy either, but that wasn't the point.

"Hey Hugo, how's it going?"

Some sort of nearly insulting nod, a semi-acknowledgment.

"Listen, are you going to be seeing Alfredo? I want to send him a message of thanks. Tell him thanks very much for the story, for being allowed to see Martín. It came out pretty well."

Hugo's eyes slid sideways to his companions, inviting them to see the humour in the way this big, paunchy gringo was sucking up to him.

"Could you do that? Please send that message to Alfredo."

"Yes, I'll do that," said Hugo, finally.

Yeah of course you will, you bastard, thought Robert, but continued anyway.

"Because, you know, the fact is I'd like to see Martín again, but this time I'd like to use a camera. Could you tell Alfredo that? I think Alfredo wanted me to use a camera. Can you tell him that?"

"I'll do that."

"Okay. Thanks. Can I get you guys something? Some more drinks."

"Yes, more drinks," said Hugo, smiling more broadly.

He paid for the soft drinks with a couple of greasy notes. The man attending behind the smeary glass counters, which covered the fly-pocked baked goods, had no expression on his round face, as if he wanted to give the impression of not really being there. This was the safest policy for the people of San Vicente. Robert didn't expect Hugo to help him but it had been worth a try.

He met the *Times* man outside the Alkalá. He looked trim and über-Californian in his sun glasses.

"Hi, Robert. I've already organised a car."

"Fine. Do you mind if I just rush up and get a drink?"

"Could you be quick? We're going to pay two hundred thousand pesos? Is that okay? Half and half, right?"

"Fine."

Robert wanted another beer but had a soft drink instead, and it was so sweet it stung. A tall, bony driver with a moustache and a square jaw was twirling car keys by the *Times* man when he got back down.

"Víctor," he said, holding out his hand. Then in a single elastic movement he leapt into his taxi and closed the door behind him.

"Los Pozos?"

"Los Pozos," said the *Times* man, revealing his faulty Spanish accent as his only apparent flaw. The guy was too perfect really. He was a type of anti-Klitsch.

A short way out of town, they took a stony dirt road into the hills. Miniature footballs dangling from the rear view mirror bounced and jerked on their nylon cord, and the taxi made juddering progress over the white rocks. Conversation was impossible. They wound up the windows against the dust, and the air was hot and barely breathable. Robert, already drained by the heat and the morning's drive, felt nauseous and wondered why he had come. But it was a pretty drive, so it felt like a sickly dream. They passed grass-filled depressions, with palm trees on the ridge above, and crinkly hills repeated into the distance like a wave running along a shaken whip. Sometimes they dipped through covered tunnels of forest, oases of shade which felt as if there should be water close by, and occasionally past groups of wooden shacks, with waving children and silent, worried adults, the old men with faces like cracked mud, their white bristles like dead grass.

At Los Pozos a large billboard, posted by the government for the benefit of those attending peace talks, listed locally endemic tropical diseases: among them malaria, elephantiasis, leishmaniasis, yellow fever, and dengue.

"I feel ill already," said Robert.

"What? Oh, yes," said the *Times* correspondent, "Let's see if we can find anybody."

They drove up past the town, which was just a few weather-stained wooden huts, and parked outside the prefabricated houses set up for the talks. The gate was locked, but Víctor bounded off to look for the caretaker, a local man who approached them with slow, plodding steps, carrying a small radio playing Vallenato.

"There's nobody here," said the caretaker, clasping the radio to his ear.

"Yes, we can see that. Do you know if they're coming this afternoon?"

"The people from the FARC are coming, I think."

He was mumbling, it was hard to hear him.

"In about how long?"

"Soon, any moment now."

"Oh shit," said the *Times* correspondent. "I suppose that could mean in ten minutes or two hours or not at all. Why don't we wait here a while and see what happens? There's nothing better to do in San Vicente."

So they sat down on a wooden bench inside a small open kiosk outside the wire fences. It was late afternoon now and the day was beginning to cool down.

"What do you make of this circus?" asked the *Times* man.

Robert leaned back against the bench.

"Yeah, the talks are a circus all right," he said, "But I don't see why the FARC should want to end it. I think going back to the bush would be a shock for them."

"Good. I'm wanted back in Bogota by Friday. It's my youngest's birthday, so I'll be in big trouble if I'm not there."

The *Times* correspondent had brought a pretty American wife and two pretty children with him to Colombia. Robert used to see them around sometimes, in shopping malls or restaurants. The woman looked elegant and nervous. She was probably just shy, but good-looking enough to be taken for arrogant.

"How does your wife like it here?" he asked.

"She doesn't. Colombia's not really her thing. She was a lawyer back home, and here she's just looking after the kids. Of course it's only a few years, she understands that."

"It's tough on the family. This correspondent thing."

"How about yourself?"

"I've got a daughter back in England. As I say, it's tough this business."

"That's too bad."

"Yup."

"There's nothing more important than your family. I couldn't imagine being separated from my kids. That's one sacrifice I'm not prepared to make."

Robert said, "It wasn't a sacrifice I was prepared to make either. It was me who got sacrificed."

"Is that right? I'm sorry. Hey, that was a great interview of yours by the way, the guerrilla from Chicago. That kid's got himself into a mess."

They waited until the shadows lengthened before the *Times* man had to admit the impossibility of work that day and then they went and found Víctor limbering up by his taxi. The drive down the curving road was more tolerable in the cool of evening. The *Times* man put his dark glasses back on because of the low angle of the setting sun and the lenses reflected splinters of gold.

At dinner at the Toro Negro, Robert ordered chicken with salad and chips in order to make a change from the steak and salad and chips he had had for lunch, and drank five or six beers, losing count as he ordered them. After the meal, a decision was taken to walk as a group to La Playa, which was a strip of sandy beach along the River Caquetá where a couple of late-night huts sold drinks and the locals went dancing sometimes. They walked for about twenty minutes down a dark road through the jungle and across a hill, stumbling over stones in the starlight.

"Isn't this exactly what you're not supposed to do in Colombia? I mean walk around in the country in the pitch dark?" said an American woman.

Someone else said, "Just watch out for the land mines. As long as you don't step on one of those, you'll be okay."

They drank beer at the beach but, as it was a river shore, it was dirty, and they were uncomfortable on the sand in case something bit them. On the far bank they could see a few black hills and the occasional glowing light, maybe peasants, maybe the FARC. Instead of the feeling of freedom of being next to the ocean, La Playa had the same trapped continental air as the rest of San Vicente, despite its name. The whole place was a dump. Until the peace talks, it had hardly existed on the map of Colombia, except as a heat shimmer on the fringe of the Amazon. Now it was a dump refracted through television, but that wouldn't last.

"Hey, does anyone want to dance?" asked the American woman.

"Dance?" said the burly, long-haired photographer. "Did you say dance?"

"Fuck, yeah, dance!"

And the two of them stood up on the sand, moving to the distorted sound of a ghetto blaster propped by one of the booze stalls. The photographer made a joke of it, but the woman seemed to enjoy herself anyway.

The blond photographer, who was leaning on the sand next to Robert, laughed and sang in a low voice, "American woman, stay away from me, American woman, mamma let me be."

Then he said, "Boy, I knew there was a reason I came to Colombia."

Klitsch was there, with his shirt unbuttoned, swigging out of a shared bottle of rum. He looked like a tramp. He looked like he stank.

The walk back under the stars was more pleasant than being on the beach itself. They were always almost lost but it was more funny than frightening. Then they reached the first little concrete houses of San Vicente, lit by naked electric bulbs, and it was depressing again to see the locals sitting on their front doorsteps, waiting until it was cool enough to sleep.

Robert went into his baking, blood-coloured cell in the Alkalá and turned on the fan. He was sweaty but couldn't face a cold shower before bed so he just washed his face. It was almost midnight but he dialled home.

Milena answered the phone and sounded sleepy.

"I can't bear being without you," she said. "I'm all alone here."

"Good."

"What do you mean, good?"

"I don't want you seeing anyone else."

"Come back soon. Please."

"I want to. I want to now. I miss you," he said.

After speaking to Milena, he was able to sleep. He stayed in San Vicente for three more days until it was clear that the peace talks would survive, and then he drove back to Florencia with Pacho and took a plane to Bogota. A month later he heard Víctor the taxi driver had been killed by someone on the road just outside San Vicente and his car set on fire. He thought about doing a story about taxi drivers and the way they worked with journalists covering the conflict, but he had to conclude that it wouldn't sell.

Ten

"I love you."

"Why? Why do you love me?"

"Because you're beautiful, intelligent. Because I need you."

"Because you need me, that's it."

"Don't be like that. What's wrong? Don't you love me?"

"Oh, you are silly. Of course I do."

"Well, give me a kiss."

"No."

"Come on."

"No."

"Why not?"

"If you love me, why do you talk to me like that?"

Milena sat with her back as straight as a yogi's, holding her freshly-painted profile rigid. She had crashed his new Toyota on her return from a visit to her beautician. Robert had paid for her to take driving lessons to give her something to do and she had finished them less than a week earlier. He was getting used to that hard, perfect face. It never failed to put him in his place: that of supplicant. But soon she relented. She always did. Out of affection or good-heartedness.

"It wasn't my fault. I was scared."

"Poor thing."

"I didn't crash the car on purpose."

"I always knew you didn't, darling."

"That imbecile came over the hill and I wasn't looking because I was trying to change the CD and it didn't work because you were too afraid to ask them to fix it."

"I wasn't afraid."

"Yes you were. You were ashamed to take it back and get them to fix it. I don't know why. You're timid sometimes."

"Never mind. Give me a kiss."

"No."

"Why not?"

"Because you make me angry."

"Jesus Christ, it was you who crashed the car. How can you be angry with me?"

"Because you were too scared to get the CD player fixed."

She was capricious in a girlish, not a malicious, way. She took comfort in it. Then she laughed.

"I am silly, aren't I?"

"Yes, you are, getting angry with me because you crashed the car."

"No I'm not."

And so on.

Robert was always worried that she would get bored living with him. She had postponed her studies in her hometown to come and stay with him in Bogota and didn't know anyone in the city except for a few relatives she wanted to avoid, so she had nothing to do except to go shopping and watch soap operas on television. At first she seemed perfectly content with this, rather to Robert's surprise. She would spend hours arranged elegantly on his stain-coloured sofa, sipping fruit juices mixed with milk as, on the screen, telenovela maids became mistresses or poisoned their lesbian lovers or broke out of jail, and the swaying patches of light from the lounge-room window, which faced the patio bordered by trees, faded from lime to lily to lilac. But after a few weeks she began to get restless. She would come and stand over him as he tried to work in his untidy study, hugging him with her slender arms from behind, and then sulk if he didn't start some affectionate chat or make love or take her for an ice cream or for a drive or to the cinema.

"You've got to do something with yourself," he said after a few weeks, but this offended her.

"You mean I'm just leeching off you. You resent me."

"No, I don't mean that. I mean for your own good. You must be pretty tired of hanging around the house all day, and I'm not much fun. I've got to earn money, so I can't talk to you all the time."

She flounced off into the bedroom and slammed the door.

The next day, Milena made a show of strength. She forced him to sack his cleaner, who had made the mistake of not addressing her with the respectful title *doña*. At first, Robert refused to fire her. He said he had a responsibility to her as a mother with a family to support.

"She thinks I'm just some slut you picked up," said Milena.

"No she doesn't. That's completely unfair."

"So you don't care if she thinks I'm a slut? She matters to you more than I do? Have you slept with her? Is that it? What's she like in bed?"

Robert was often amazed at how badly Milena was prepared to suppose he might behave.

"Are you mad? Have you ever looked at the woman?"

She slammed the bedroom door.

The next day Robert's voice trembled and tears slid down the cleaner's chubby face as he gave her two months' wages in severance pay.

Yet Milena, cruel as Caligula when threatened, was also very sentimental. Her eyes would occasionally moisten when, on their way to a restaurant or shopping mall, they passed beggar women wrapped up with their babies on the street, and, if a television station asked for donations for an operation on some sick child singled out for cuteness, a marrow transplant or expensive chemotherapy, she unfailingly noted down the bank details to send money, sometimes actually doing so. Images of childhood in general affected her. She kept a midget teddy bear, in a teeny pink dress, chained to a key ring in her purse.

One night, they attended a party at the house of a British journalist in the old part of town. Robert always liked arriving at places with Milena. He liked seeing how people looked at her. But then the problem was that they kept looking at her, especially the men, and he liked that less.

"Where'd you get her?" asked a tall, ginger-haired free-lancer.

Robert didn't really want to answer.

"Where'd you get yours?" he responded.

"Jumble sale. No, really!"

Before he could explain, the girlfriend of the ginger-haired journalist took him by the arm and tugged him away towards the darkest corner of the crowded lounge.

Robert was drawn into conversation with an American newspaper correspondent. With the exception of the cool climate, the party was like being at the Alkalá. The crowd was mainly the same. There were quite a lot of Colombians but the gringo element predominated, so people were drinking beer and talking instead of drinking rum and dancing. The messy, cramped house was situated on a dodgy street in the mountains and Robert wondered whether the Toyota, with its bumper bar now crumpled like a crooked smile, would still be there when they went to look for it.

"What I think about the peace process ... what, what I, what ...," said the newspaper correspondent, "Hello."

Milena had brought Robert another beer. He put his arm around her.

"William Wilcox."

"Milena Marulanda," she replied.

"Marulanda? Like, like, old whatsisname, old thingy?"

Milena did not speak English but she guessed what he meant and replied in Spanish.

131

"Yes, like Manuel Marulanda. It is not his real name, but unfortunately he chose that name when he started the FARC. It's my real name so it's embarrassing for me."

"Well, it doesn't have to be embarrassing," said the American. "It's just a name. You know, it's a funny thing about Colombia, but I don't think I've ever been anywhere with so few family names to go round. Why is that?"

"I suppose a few conquistadors got lucky," said Robert, speaking English despite Milena's presence, out of laziness. The American continued in his version of Spanish.

"And what do you think about the FARC, señorita Marulanda?"

He meant that last touch to be comic.

"They killed my father," said Milena.

"Oh. Oh shit," said the American, "I'm sorry."

To change the subject, he asked her where she was from and she told him. But he had had too much to drink, and couldn't contain his surprise at her answer.

"And what the hell were you doing down there? I mean, you know."

She shrugged. "I was studying."

"Studying? That's a pretty funny place to study."

"Not everyone has a choice," said Robert, speaking Spanish this time, and that killed off that conversation. Later Robert chatted to a very slim and good-looking woman with short blond hair who worked at the Canadian embassy. She was speaking about recent Colombian literature and generously tried to involve Milena.

132

"Did you read that?" she asked, in reference to a well-known title.

"No," said Milena.

"But what about *La Virgen de los Sicarios*?"

"No," said Milena, smiling sweetly. "I don't know much about books."

"I didn't like it much," said Robert, "It was histrionic."

"What?"

"Hysterical. Exaggerated. What I mean is that it was no good."

He pulled Milena towards him.

"Oh, I don't know," said the Canadian. "It reflects reality. Reality in Colombia is pretty over the top, people do get killed like that, for nothing, and that's pretty upsetting, so maybe that's why you think the prose style is exaggerated. To me it was real, emotionally real."

"What do you think?" asked Milena, looking at Robert with wide eyes.

"I think I want to give you a kiss."

"Come on. That's not an answer," said the Canadian.

The stars were shining as brightly as the streetlamps as they walked up a hill towards the car. Robert felt the chill air clear his woozy head, but he still felt pretty merry from all the beer he had drunk. He tried to take Milena's hand but she wouldn't let him.

"Why did you say that?" she said.

"Why did I say what?"

"You know what you said."

133

"No I don't. I honestly don't."

He had that Stalinist show-trial feeling again.

"Why did you say I was poor?"

"I didn't."

"Why did you say to that man that I didn't have a choice? That's the same thing. You're embarrassed by me. You're embarrassed by where I'm from."

A family of recyclers was sorting through rubbish outside a house fenced by barbed wire, piling cardboard and bottles in a cart. Their horse, mangy and skinny-ribbed, waited with its long neck lolling down, and a toddler, rugged up to the eyeballs so he or she looked like a stuffed doll, was tottering around with a Coke can. It wasn't safe to argue on the street at night.

"You know that's not true," said Robert. "I was defending you."

"I don't need you to defend me."

The car was still there, he was happy to see. Nearby, beside a sentry box, stood a night watchman with an old, wooden-butted rifle. He wore a thick woollen poncho against the cold and his face was covered by a balaclava beneath his peaked cap, with slits for his eyes, nose and mouth.

The car beeped and clicked when Robert pressed the button on his keyring, and the doors hissed as the seals closed. It was as if they had climbed into a portable first world. Looking outside at the poor people in the night was like seeing them on television. Milena put on a CD. It was a song by Moby, "We are made of stars", and Robert listened as he drove into the mountains, in sight of the huge glowing spread of a shanty town on a far hill, its distant lamps, fed by pirated electricity and marking out the territory of rival gangs, twinkling like fairy lights.

"I don't want you to go back ever," said Robert.

He was surprised by his own words. He often took decisions like that. They weren't the result of analysis. They were born fully formed, and logical justification came afterwards.

"What do you mean?"

"I want you to stay," he said, "And I want you to know that. So you can make plans."

"What sort of plans, Robert?"

He took a long, easy curve, driving with his back straight, keeping his eyes fixed on an imaginary centre point in the road. He was a little drunk after all so it was better to be careful.

"I just want you to have a life here," he said.

"A life?"

"Yes. You know," he said, "I just don't want you to have to worry about going back. I want this to be permanent."

Once they got home they had sex, which might have been okay to look at, but it was a bit anaesthetised. Afterwards, he lay in bed next to her and thought to himself "this isn't too bad". She was sleeping on her side and he could see the shape of her hips under the sheet. Light from a streetlamp was filtering in through a gap in the curtains. She smelt like sour milk. He didn't want her to go, he knew that much.

That was definite. But she was with him because of money, he knew that too. That, at least, was the origin of their relationship. He knew it clearly, now that he took the trouble to think about it. But so what? So what? That's what it's all about, he thought. Need – it's inevitable. A baby doesn't want its mother because of her personality. It's because without her it would die. It's evolutionary and you can't be ashamed of evolution. But it's still love. You can't say it's not love because it isn't disinterested. Perhaps there's no such thing. And Milena was the perfect woman, at least physically: a veritable Barbie doll made flesh. He didn't want a pen pal. He didn't want to start a book of the month club or trade haikus. She had a good heart. Over time they'd have more to talk about too, the more experience they accumulated together, the more their aims coincided. They'd have plenty to chat about. Restrict your objectives and you will obtain them.

Boozy thoughts, but clear as moonlight. Responding to a kind of electric excitement, he got out of bed and padded quietly out of the room and into the lounge, where he sat on the sofa in his underwear, feeling its textile covering cool against his back and looking at the dark, slow-moving shape of a tree. He didn't have much, he thought; he didn't have much in his life. The tree shadow moved suddenly on the wall, snapping like a dragon at something that wasn't there. It was hard to understand how he'd got where he was, to Bogota, Colombia, high up on a mountainous plateau, far away from what had been his family, his language. How the fuck had he got there, he thought. What had he been trying to get away from? He had almost forgotten his original motivations but they still carried him forward in the same old attitudes. It wasn't money, that's for sure, so what was it? Was it experience? Well, he'd had plenty of that. He carried on as if he had a purpose. He had plenty of opinions but had mostly forgotten why. He was a type of robot man, something with a cardboard box instead of a head, moved by the wind.

Let's simplify things, he thought, in his nearly naked state, feeling slightly cold now. I should concentrate on Milena. And he felt sorry. He felt sorry, too, for himself and for his little girl in London.

He got up and stood at the window. Two different types of colourless light, from the stars and the streetlamps, illuminated the patio and the trees, like a lamp behind an X-ray sheet.

Over the next few days everything went swimmingly. Everything was just fine and dandy.

On his first morning with Milena after deciding he wanted to live with her in a permanent way, he rose early, rustled her up some nice scrambled eggs, and then, solicitous and affectionate throughout, tried to make love to her. He couldn't, but, never mind, he was tired and he'd done it the night before and he was almost forty years old after all.

The 12-o'clock sky was a faded denim of pale clouds as they drove through the mountains in their lopsided Toyota. They stopped at a roadside restaurant for lunch.

Milena wanted chunchullo. Robert asked for steak, chips and guacamole. She drank Coke and he had a beer.

Her crispy tubes of fried gut sizzled in their half-ringlets. His gristled rump curled in a sooty sheen of oil beside a guano-pat of avocado. Clutching paper plates they sat on very green grass, beneath what had become a very blue sky. Primary colours, like an old ad for a brand of photographic film from the days when people still expected black-and-white, when red and yellow or green were surprising in an image. Milena, despite her lack of sleep, looked glossy, slightly more than human.

"I never believed I could be so happy," she said.

What could you say about that? Happy was one of those words, like love, which it was better not to explain. It was better just to repeat them.

Robert drank some beer, tangy out of the can.

"Everything's perfect, isn't it?" he said. "I mean, just look where we are. It's like we're in a movie, isn't it?"

It was an image of emotional dislocation, but he meant it in a positive way, and Milena liked it.

"You're the hero," she said.

"I don't think so. But you could definitely be in a film."

"You sound like Pacho."

"It's true."

The air was cool and Alpine but the too-blue sky was beaming equatorial radiation. Robert felt he was in a high-altitude microwave, burning without heat. He adjusted his forelock, hoping to cover more of his reddening brow.

"What are you going to do about your studies?" he asked.

"I don't care. It doesn't matter to me so long as I'm with you."

"You've got to do something with yourself."

"Why?"

"That's a good question. A very good question."

"If you want me to work, I can find a job."

"I don't want you to work."

"Well then."

"I want you to look after me," he said.

They had only been together for a little more than a month, and Robert had already practically proposed to her. It was disorienting but not unpleasant as he sat frying in the sun next to his beautiful girl. It wasn't so much like being in a film, as he had said; it was more like watching a film, in which he only knew the characters in a superficial way, so that he never knew what they were going to do next.

In the afternoon, as his sunburn ripened and matured, they drove around looking for things to do. At his suggestion, they went to a museum in the centre of Bogota, but Milena didn't like that. Then they walked around the narrow streets of the old part of town, where they were trailed by beggars. Robert's head began to ache. When it got dark they drove back to the city's more affluent quarter and it was time to eat again. Then they slept.

How else to say it? Happy. That's what they were.

Eleven

He hadn't given up hope of doing another story on Martín, this time with pictures, with video – the full deal, but Pacho's go-between with Alfredo, who had arranged their first trip, had disappeared. Robert had never met the guy, who was just someone Pacho knew in Medellin. Pacho had got his number by luck from someone else he'd known and, for almost two years, they would agree to clandestine meetings at a shop on the frontiers of a slum which served fried empanadas and black coffee in plastic cups, with plastic straws to stir the sugar in.

The meetings were regular because you have to keep your contacts warm, and, if Pacho wasn't working on a story, he'd give the guy the impression that he was. They'd smoke ciga-rettes and chat in low voices and his contact would keep looking over his shoulder. Then one day he didn't show up and he had also stopped answering his cellphone and that was the end of that. He might have been arrested. He might have left the city or changed his number. Or Pacho or Robert might simply have fallen from favour. Being an illegal organ-isation, the FARC could be as inaccessible as it wanted to be. It was impossible to tell.

Robert had tried sending Martín an e-mail using the address he had given him, but there was no way of knowing whether he had even seen it. There was access to Internet in San Vicente, but Martín might not even be there, he could be anywhere. Of course, Robert could try going down to San Vicente to see if he could talk his way into a meeting with Alfredo, but, if for some reason they didn't want to see him any more, he could waste weeks there without getting a reply. They would just tell him to wait, and nothing would ever happen.

So Robert called Alvaro Pardo, a friend, or rather associate of his, a Colombian journalist known, and, in some quarters, disliked, for his good contacts with the FARC. They arranged to have lunch in an Argentine restaurant in La Candelaria, and Robert found him already seated beneath a dark brick wall decorated with black-and-white pictures of tango singers and old Buenos Aires football teams.

Pardo wanted to celebrate his most recent scoop: an interview with a Japanese businessman the rebels were holding for ransom. They had had him for more than a year and wanted an unrealistic amount of money for his release. This was an excellent story for Pardo, because, although of little interest to the wider world, he had been able to sell the video to Japanese television for several tens of thousands of dollars. It was comforting for Robert to talk about that sort of subject in terms of money. Journalism could be a very dirty business, but Pardo saw things practically. They ordered a bottle of red wine and Robert asked about the spirits in which he had found the Japanese businessman.

Pardo smiled. Like many journalists, he was a naturally genial man, and, although his features, his nose and cheeks, had swollen and reddened slightly over the years, he still had what could be called a boyish face. But his hair was white, so he looked ten years older than his forty-five years, and his easy good humour would very occasionally, but suddenly and without warning, vanish to reveal a morbid sensitivity to criticism.

"Well, actually, the Japanese guy was sad to see me go," he said, "But that's only natural. And it's not my fault he was kidnapped. I was only doing a story."

"Of course. That's your job," repeated Robert, drinking his wine. Pardo was enjoying the subject. It was a triumph for him, and not only profitable.

"I brought him some cigarettes and some magazines. I got him some of those, you know, Manga, those dirty comics the Japanese like so much. They're a strange people, the Japanese, so correct, so proper, and they read that filth."

"Manga," said Robert.

"And he was glad of someone to talk to. His Spanish isn't up to much, and the guerrillas aren't very accomplished, how shall I say, conversationalists. You should see the way they're keeping him. It was a sort of pen. He cried when I left. I promised to call his wife, and I did that straight away when I got back. But her English was worse than his, so I don't know if it was a comfort to her."

142

Robert toasted Pardo's success and suggested they order food. Pardo was in no hurry. The restaurant was full of businessmen in suits making the best of their lunch hour, but he was drinking wine and smoking and enjoying himself.

"I want one of every nationality," he said. "It's the same story, but I can sell it every time. I want an American, an Englishman, and then I'll sell the interviews to newspapers in the U.S. and Britain, and I can live for a year off that."

Robert always tried to be hearty with Pardo, but they never quite clicked. There was always an emptiness behind their conversations, a tension just waiting to emerge. Pardo said they should get a second bottle of wine. He was an even better drinker than Robert was.

Robert had meant to introduce the subject of Martín carefully, but he had drunk more than half a bottle of wine now on an empty stomach and it made him reckless. So he just said, "I want to see that guy again. I want to do it properly this time."

"Who?" asked Pardo, and, when Robert told him, he said, "What an arsehole. Not letting you take his photo. Wasting your time like that."

The waiter served their steaks. They were very big and Robert wasn't hungry any more because the wine had filled him up. It had also made him sentimental.

"It must be tough for a guy like that," he said, "For Martín, I mean. He's an American, and he's not used to all that. He doesn't even speak the language that well, for Christ's sake. He's just some idiot kid. And now he can't

143

leave or it would be desertion and they'd shoot him."

"What do you mean? Why is it tough for him in particular?"

"You're right," said Robert. There was a tango playing. He liked tango. The song was sad but arrogant at the same time.

"They're fighting a war," said Pardo, "Why should he be any different just because he's a gringo?"

"It's just he's so far from home," said Robert, "But you're right."

"Far from home," repeated Pardo, "Far from home." He laughed with his mouth full of food. "You're far from home too, Hoggard my friend. Yes you are."

"And, you know, I am," said Robert, "But at least I'm not stuck in the jungle like that idiot. And they're never going to win that stupid war. It's just a business."

Pardo closed his eyes deliberately, just for a second, and took a deep breath.

"It is not a business," he said, "It's complicated but you shouldn't be too cynical. It's not just a business."

"Oh come on, it is a business."

Robert was making a joke of it, and it really seemed funny to him at the time. He drank some more of his wine.

"No, no, it's not," said Pardo, "You can't reduce it just to that."

"It is a business, but it's just not very profitable," said Robert.

"Except for us, my friend, except for us," said Pardo, and they clinked glasses.

And then Robert thought he may as well ask the question he'd come to ask. It seemed as good a time as any.

"Hey, Alvaro, is there any chance you help me with Alfredo so I can see Martín?"

Alvaro looked at him. His smile broadened.

"Ah my friend," he said, and smiled and raised his glass again. That was all that Robert got out of him. He didn't say anything else about it.

After the meal, they went to a car park and got into Pardo's old Renault and he lit a marijuana cigarette and put on a bootleg cassette which he said had been given to him by a FARC guerrilla who had stolen it off the Internet. The first song was *Airbag*, by Radiohead, and Robert was surprised by his up-to-date taste in music.

"The guy just played it and I loved it. It stayed in my head. So he gave me a copy," said Pardo, "But I can't understand the English. Tell me what it means, Hoggard."

They drove down the Séptima and took turns to drag on the marijuana. There was a lot of traffic and the sky was grey, but it didn't bother them. Robert tried to translate the song but wasn't very good at it.

"*He vuelto para salvar al universo*," he said.

"What do they mean by that?" asked Pardo.

"I don't know."

"*Una bolsa de aire me salvó la vida y he nacido de nuevo.*"

"What a load of crap," said Pardo, "But it sounds …"

"It sounds good," said Robert.

Twelve

It was Sunday morning and he went into the bedroom just as Milena was coming out of the shower, bound up in towels, her long hair covered by a fluffy blue turban. He tried to unwrap her with a single, elegant flick of the wrist, but she pushed him away.

"Don't. I'm in a hurry. I'm going to mass."

"Mass? Really?"

"Yes, why not? What's funny?"

"No, not funny. Not funny at all. Are you going to confess?"

"I should," she said, "and so should you."

"I'm not Catholic."

"Hmph. You should be. Everybody should be."

"I had no idea you'd want to go to mass."

"That doesn't surprise me."

"What do you mean by that?"

"Are you an atheist?"

She was frowning now.

"Oh, I don't know," said Robert. "No, not really, I suppose. It's not something I think about much."

"Well, at least you're not an atheist."

Since she had gained access to Robert's credit card, her wardrobe had expanded to cope with the cooler season. To go to Church she got dressed up to look sexier than usual, although the lipstick she selected was more matt than gloss. She put on quite a short skirt and a tight-fitting grey jumper. She wore black stockings and black high-heeled shoes with tiny bows. Most days she just wore jeans.

"Will you come with me?" she said, addressing him from inside a cloud of perfume.

"Okay, I'll walk you there. But I won't go in."

"Why not?"

"I don't believe in it. It would be hypocritical."

It was a very bright morning, with just a few clouds which set off the polished-glass sky. The red brick buildings and neat, well-tended parks looked small and plastic, and even the dark green mountains seemed to close the scene, reducing rather than increasing its scale. Walking by Milena's side, in her slipstream of scent, Robert felt jealous of everyone, even the priest. He kissed her on the cheek before she entered the church, so he wouldn't smear her lipstick, and watched her nicely curved backside as she made a little curtsey to the altar and crossed herself before taking to her pew. There were a lot of people in the church, all dressed up. The women wore skirts, the men wore suits and ties.

There were some beggars hanging around outside the building. One had no legs and moved around by using his hands to push along a sort of home-made skateboard.

There was also a big old man, with huge hands and a square jaw, who stood looking at his feet, holding out a plastic cup.

Robert gave a few hundred pesos to one of them, who shouted "Lord bless you!" and he walked quickly away and down to the Parque de la 93. It was still early, so there were cleaners sweeping up broken bottles from the Saturday night festivities. A few coffee shops were open, selling big breakfasts with maize griddle cakes and omelettes or scrambled eggs mixed with tomato and onion, but there was a sour smell from the rubbish spilt on the street.

He bought *El Tiempo* from a woman at some traffic lights and looked at the front page, which had a story about the foreign debt and a big headline about the spread of AIDS. Nothing he could see which he had missed, but nothing he would like to follow up either. He didn't really enjoy reading the Colombian papers, so he folded it up and headed back up the hill, crossing a main road. The church was a large, modern, triangular construction, mainly an angled roof with hardly any building under it. He positioned himself where he could see the entrance but was out of begging range, and read the article about AIDS. There was, as usually turns out to be the case with that sort of story, a lot of it about, and more of it all the time. Mass was ending, and people were shuffling out to the sound of organ music. He caught Milena's eye and she smiled at him. She looked proud.

"Do you have something for this man?" she asked, indicating the legless skateboarder, and Robert handed her a five-hundred-peso coin and she gave it to the beggar.

"How was it?"

She gave him her arm and they began to walk home.

"I feel better. It had been a long time since I had gone to Mass."

"Did you confess?"

"No. But I will the next time. I want to take communion."

"What do you have which you need to confess?"

"Why are you so interested? That's for the priest, not you. I've got enough to need to confess it."

"About me?"

"No. Why would it be about you?"

"No, no reason," he said. He put his arm around her shoulders and squeezed.

He had been slumming journalistically and had sold a series of very easy stories on the oil industry, so he was relatively flush with cash and they went to lunch at a restaurant that was expensive by Bogota standards. He was becoming aware that joint consumption was their principal shared activity. They sat down at a table by the window and ordered drinks and looked at the menu. Milena was in a good mood and chatted quite happily about going to Mass. Then she started talking about her family again, about how her mother was so superstitious, and how, once, when she was a little girl, she had been taken to a faith healer, who had rubbed her stomach and that immediately she had felt better but it was probably only a coincidence.

Robert drank white wine and wondered, with sudden impatience, how much he really knew about her. He tried

149

to control himself, but then he gave in, and smiled and took her hand and said, "You know, I was reading this story about HIV in *El Tiempo*. There's so much of it about. And most people who have it don't know they have it, so they spread it around and don't take the drugs until it's too late."

"That's terrible," said Milena.

"Isn't it?" said Robert.

"I've never met anyone who's had HIV."

"What you mean is that you've never met anyone who's known they have HIV and has told you that they have it."

"That's true."

And she shivered.

"Have you ever had a test?" he asked.

He couldn't help it. He really wanted to know the answer.

"No. Why should I?"

"No reason. Of course not. I'm just asking. I just wondered if you'd ever worried about it and had a test."

"No. No, I haven't. Have you?"

"Well, you know, I'm certain I haven't got it. I have a kid, so I'd know if I had it."

Milena said, "Maybe I should have a test, just to put ourselves at ease."

"Well, it couldn't hurt."

Robert felt much better now that Milena had said that, and he was extremely nice to her for all the rest of the meal.

They were always telling each other they loved each

other, and over the next few days they did so more than ever. He told her he loved her and asked her if she loved him and she said yes. This happened several times a day, sometimes several times in an hour. As a special concession, because he didn't feel too comfortable about the situation he had put her in and wanted to make amends, he took her to a film she wanted to see and which he had previously resisted. He was more concerned than ever by the idea she might get bored, but was still at a loss about what to do about it. She had no friends, no job, didn't study, didn't like reading. She just watched television, and ate, and shopped, and slept with him. It was this very passive inactivity which almost led him, several times, finally, explicitly, to propose to her. Marriage would give her something to do. He almost said it two or three times, only just pulling back.

She went to the doctor's alone to request an AIDS test. Robert hadn't accompanied her because he had thought that that would make it seem as if he was forcing her to do it. The results would not be ready until the next day, and they had a better time than usual that evening. They ordered a takeaway meal from a restaurant and ate it with a bottle of wine and then watched a DVD, cuddling on the sofa. With more intensity and frequency than usual, Milena said she loved him, and he responded in kind. Then they had defiantly prophylacticless sex and she clung to him afterwards in bed.

The next day she went early to get the results and when she got back he didn't want to ask her what they were, because he didn't want to seem worried about it. She went to make a cup of coffee. But, before she had finished, she came back from the kitchen, and said: "It was negative, by the way."

"Oh, the test? Oh, good," said Robert, "I was sure it would be. What do you want to do for lunch?"

He wanted to change the subject. That whole thing was something they could forget about. Things were okay now.

But Milena wouldn't let it drop.

"Robert?" she said.

"Yes?"

"Can I say something a little bit strong, a little bit heavy?"

"Of course you can, darling."

"You think I'm a whore, don't you?"

"No."

"Yes you do. You think I was a whore and I saw you in the town and saw my chance and took it. A rich foreign journalist, easy pickings. That's what you think, isn't it?"

He didn't say anything. The kettle began to whistle.

"Yes you do. It's so easy for you, for you foreigners. It's not your country and you don't understand."

"What do you mean?" he asked.

"You think I was a whore, don't you? That I sold myself?"

He shook his head.

"You do, don't you?"

Then he turned away. He didn't know what to do.

"The kettle," he said.

"Just tell me the truth. Go on. I won't be offended."

Her tone had changed. It was loving again. She touched him on the shoulder.

"Tell me the truth."

She kissed him on the side of the neck. The whistling top shot off the kettle with a clang.

"Go on. Ask me," she said.

He shook his head.

"Ask me. Milena, were you a whore?"

"No," he said.

"Go on. What would you do if you asked me and I said yes?"

"I'd still love you."

She began to cry.

"But you do think that, don't you? You do," she said.

In the evening, for perhaps the fortieth time that day, he told Milena that he loved her. The words weren't a real type of communication, they weren't meant to convey any new information; it was more the physical fact of their sound that mattered. But then their relationship had never had much to do with words; language had been just one of several elements tapping out its emotional rhythm, its slow dance from need to comfort.

She didn't reply anyway.

"Why don't you say something to me?" he said.

The light of the fast-setting sun was reflected, via the critical angle of a windowpane, as a tiny bonfire in her perfectly opaque brown eyes. The skin of her face, coated carefully with olive-pink foundation, seemed in the fading glow to have acquired statue-like significance, that false aura of meaning imparted by beauty.

"I love you," he said again.

Sliding his arm along the superior rim of the sofa he ran it over her shoulder.

"Don't you believe me?" he said, and she shrugged him off.

It wasn't the right question and he knew it.

Thirteen

The next morning he checked his inbox and there was a message from Martín. He had never really believed the guy would reply to him, but, now that he had, Robert didn't feel like opening it. He hadn't slept and he didn't care what the guy had to say. He half-wanted to delete it and go back to bed. He went into the kitchen and made himself a mug of instant coffee. He hadn't got dressed yet or had a shower and he was still in his underpants. He had thought Milena was still asleep when he got up, but he saw now that she had closed the bedroom door.

An e-mail was such a banal thing for a rebel to send, he thought. He probably got spam too. Then, with distaste, Robert remembered the message he had sent the guy several weeks earlier. A standard plea for an interview, it had concluded with the words *Trust me*. That was a joke, he thought. Then he sat down at his laptop and opened the mail. There wasn't much to it after all, just a couple of sentences. And it signed off *Jesse Sojka*.

His real name. Was that trust, thought Robert? And then he thought about what Martín had written: "You may be surprised, but I think we can still be of use to each other."

Robert sent a quick reply and then went into the bedroom to get some clothes. Milena was lying very still in bed and she had drawn the blankets up over her face. She was breathing very quietly, and the room was heavy with the smell of both of them. Robert stood watching her for a few seconds and then he put his clothes over his arm and left the bedroom, shutting the door carefully behind him. He got dressed in the living room, in a corner by the sofa, where he was out of sight of the window. Then he went out of the flat and walked out onto the street. He had no destination in mind. The sky was grey and it looked like it could drizzle. He crossed the road and went up to the entrance of a park and looked at the trees, but didn't stop or go in. He had his hands in his pockets and walked as fast as he could. It was a working day and there were plenty of people about, but he would have liked to have walked somewhere where he could avoid them. He crossed a busy road and followed a canal through another park, which climbed up the mountain towards a highway. He didn't go over the highway, but went down the hill and chose a tree-lined road which would take him for as long a distance as possible without having to think of turning in another direction.

"My friend," said Pardo, when Robert answered the phone. He spoke the two words in English and chuckled, as if they were intrinsically comic, before he continued in Spanish, "I'm sorry. You know, I was just thinking, why is it that English is so impoverished a language for swearing? Fucking this, fucking that. Motherfucker. Fuck you. It's all fuck, fuck, fuck. Nothing else."

Pardo began to cough. Robert occasionally wondered what life was like for those members of the security forces assigned to bugging the phones of people like him.

"There's shit and arse and wanker," he said.

Pardo was breathing normally again.

"There you have it. It's all bodily functions. Nothing more. Spanish is far more creative. It even has a metaphysical side. Do you know what they say in Spain?"

"What?"

"I shit on God. *Me cago en díos.* Can you imagine that? I shit on God? Okay, it's still shit, but you're not just shitting, you're shitting on God. That's a big shit all right, to shit on God."

"How've you been, Alvaro?"

"Can we talk somewhere?"

They met in the centre of town in a small bar whose white enamel tables were stained by cigarette burns, and Pardo ordered beers for both of them. He looked tired. He had dark circles beneath his eyes, and there was a dull undertone to his skin. He shook a cigarette out of a pack onto the table and picked it up and lit it. Then he called the waiter back and asked him to bring an espresso at the same time as his beer. At first, when he rose to greet Robert, Pardo had been cheerful, but his mouth sagged as he leant back in his seat after his first exhalation of smoke. Robert asked if he was ill or if he had missed out on his sleep.

"You're right. I haven't been sleeping too well. I've been getting some unpleasant phone calls," he said.

"Oh yes?"

Pardo shook his head and tapped his cigarette on the ashtray. He coughed again.

"During the night," he said, "So I unplugged my phone, but that doesn't make you feel any better. You just think there's something important the bastards have got to tell you, that they might offer you another chance. I think that what I need is to get out of Bogota for a while. Go on a trip somewhere and disappear for a while."

"I shit on God," said Robert.

"What?"

"Just a joke."

Pardo smiled. But his eyes opened too wide for the effect to be reassuring.

"I've got a proposal for you. From our friends."

"Our friends?"

"Our old friends," said Pardo.

"You mean Alfredo?"

Pardo was tapping his cigarette on the tray again. He didn't look up. Robert looked around him. There weren't many people in the bar. In a corner, two men were playing chess with their heads in their hands. They looked like retirees and never raised their eyes from the board.

"You want to come?"

"Probably. What is it?"

"They want international press as well. Just one. So I suggested you."

"That's very nice of you, Alvaro. But what is it?"

There was music playing in the bar and quite a lot of noise from the heavy traffic on the street outside, but Pardo leant across the table and whispered. One of the chess players made a move and laughed, and a girl in a short skirt came into the bar, looked around for somebody who turned out not to be there and went out onto the street again. Robert had his doubts.

"You're too good a journalist to fall for that. You wouldn't let them take advantage of you," said Pardo.

"Oh, don't think I'm not grateful. Thank you very much," said Robert.

"Of course it's not just altruism on my part, you know. But you are my friend, so that's why your name came up," said Pardo. And then he looked around for the waiter again. "I've got to have another beer."

"Maybe you shouldn't smoke, with that cough."

"Maybe people should mind their own business."

"I'm sorry," said Robert. "I just meant your cough. And thanks again. Thank you very much."

The waiter brought their beers.

"Cheers," said Robert.

On the street outside the bar there was a man selling copies of laws passed by Congress. That was ironic, thought Robert. There were traffic laws and the rules for divorce printed in neat little booklets. Next to the man, a woman

159

had laid out tarot cards and astrological charts on a piece of cloth spread over the pavement, and behind them was a betting shop.

Pardo shook his hand. He looked terrible.

"It's going to be great," he said, "You'll see."

Fourteen

In an attempt at reconciliation, Robert took Milena to Cartagena to stay in an old convent refurbished as a Sofitel. Their timing was odd, because he had to leave soon on his reporting trip with Pardo, and they arrived on a Sunday morning, intending to remain only until the following evening. Before they had finished unpacking, their suitcases still open on the bed beside a leaf-framed terrace window, she said, "I'm going out."

"Where?"

She had seemed happy on the plane but her face had turned sullen as soon as they were alone.

"What's it to you?" she said.

"What do you mean, what's it to me? Tell me where you're going."

"I don't have to tell you anything."

"So why did you come here with me then?"

"Who knows."

"Please, just tell me where you're going."

"To mass."

"Then I'll go with you."

"No. Don't be silly. You don't believe in any of that nonsense."

161

So she left. That was the state they had come to. He had rationalised their relationship as being based on mutual need. In that sense, he had wanted to be moral to her. But she just didn't like him any more, and this was something she was unable or unwilling to overcome. This seemed like a betrayal to him.

He had to reply to an e-mail, so he turned on his laptop. He typed, *I can't help you,* then stopped. That wasn't going to get him anywhere, that was obvious, it would be counter-productive. So he didn't want to say it quite like that. But he wouldn't lie either. What he wanted were short, declarative sentences. Little steps of truth curving back on themselves in an Esler drawing. He erased what he had written and began again, typing, *I will do everything I can.* Thank God for ethics, he thought. Just thank God. Ethics keep you safe.

He put away the laptop and removed the suitcases from the bed and lay down. Air conditioning made places seem cleaner, as if they were washed with water and not cool air. And even the air was paid for here. He had a right to every pleasure in the place. So it wouldn't be his fault if he didn't get it. Sunlight swam in green-tinged pools on the ceiling.

He went outside. The Caribbean air trapped sunshine like honey in the old walled city. He walked around for a while and then took a cab the short distance to the brown-ish-grey sea. It didn't look like the Caribbean. He walked over the beach still wearing his sandals and sat down to

162

watch slow breakers lollop shore-wards, clasping his bare legs by the shins. A man appeared selling necklaces carved from coral. A boy was offering him a coconut with a straw to drink its waxy milk through a knothole.

It had clouded over, but he could feel the scratchy heat of UV rays. Returning to the old town, he ordered bottled water at a street café. A thunderstorm was about to arrive, and the sounds of everything seemed to move in closer: the conversations at neighbouring tables; a chair leg grating against stone, the gossip between a cigar seller and a waiter lounging against the wall. The table stood beneath a long, covered walkway, with regular arches like a cloister, opposite a church painted custard-yellow. A slender beam of sunlight fled across the paving stones from encroaching clouds, rain-heavy and dark mauve.

Then, without expecting to, he saw Milena leave the church. A flash of lightning lit the square and at that precise moment she stumbled. She was wearing a white dress and he watched her fall. He didn't try to speak to her and she adjusted her sunglasses and recovered herself and walked away. It had felt pornographic to watch. I should have restricted her to being a commodity, he thought. That's what I should have done, in emotional terms. It occurred to him that she was exactly equidistant in age between himself and his five-year-old daughter. She was seventeen years older than her and seventeen years younger than him. Yet time, he thought, will reduce the difference between us, eroding her youth as my middle age merely extends, following a flattening curve. He smiled. He was wishing for the decay of her physique, and there was no point to that.

It was getting close to lunchtime. The doorman at the hotel, dressed in a short-sleeved white shirt, smiled when he saw him. Inside the big old timber door, the entrance hall was cool and shady, decorated with orchids, delicately coloured and as improbably formed as the result of some genetic experiment.

Milena had beaten him back and left a scribbled note in their room.

Gone to the pool to sunbathe.

A pale-coloured bra hung over the back of a chair, a teasing souvenir of affection. The air conditioning was on too high, so he fiddled with the thermostat. With extraordinary speed, Robert began to sweat.

He took a can of Club Colombia from the mini-bar, wiped the top with his hand, opened it and took a long drink. Then he found himself looking at Milena's brassiere. He lifted part of it up with a finger and examined the chain of small, machine-embroidered flowers and wondered vaguely what they had to do with her. She was going to sunbathe by the pool. She would only sunbathe, because she didn't know how to swim. That would be a skill he would be able to impress her with.

He left the room. He walked with his back very straight along an open passageway that ran two stories above a garden of dark green trees and bushes. The change from the cool air of the room to the warmth outside was as sudden as if he had swum from deep water into a patch of shallow sea heated by the sun over white sand. The green light of the afternoon sun through the trees shifted with the breeze. There was a rich smell of flowers and soil. A maid in a white uniform smiled at him as he passed the lift and trotted down the stairs.

We can go for a walk and find a restaurant for lunch, he thought, more optimistically now. We can find just any old place and that will be fun. And then, maybe, we can come back to the hotel for a siesta and that will be more effective than talking.

At the bottom of the stairs, he turned and walked past the cushioned wicker chairs outside the dining room, and then he recognised William Wilcox coming towards him, carrying a laptop and holding his chin up as he walked, as if he was trying to read something written beneath the visor of his baseball cap.

Robert wasn't particularly happy to see him, but William grinned in greeting.

"Hey Robert, uh, nice to see you. What's up?"

"William. Just taking a few days off. And you?"

Robert saw the guy's skinny white legs descending from branded Bermudas.

"I've been out at Ciudad Nelson Mandela, you know, the shanty town, and I thought I might as well just stay here and write the story. You know, suffering." And then he added, "Jesus, they live like shit, it's really something."

Robert knew he should chat a bit, or even suggest they have a drink, but he didn't, and William was too smug to be snubbed anyway.

"Ah, well, I hope you have a nice time."

"Thanks Robert. You too. See you around."

Robert continued on his way past hotel shops, painted deep ochre, which sold overpriced local artworks. He found Milena at her ease on a deck chair in the shimmering light of the pool area. She was lying on her stomach but had raised herself up on her elbows.

There was someone else. Crouching by Milena's side, like a perspiring Punch in a Hawaiian shirt, was Klitsch.

Klitsch was just drunk enough not to be annoyed at Robert for butting in.

"Hey, it's Sir Robert Hoggard. How do you do, sire?"

Robert was in no mood for Klitsch. He looked at Milena who looked back at him with a smile, her dark eyes blank and cruel. Then she looked at Klitsch.

"What do you mean, Jacob?" said Robert.

"What I mean is," said Klitsch, smiling at Milena as she smiled at him and speaking English so she wouldn't understand, "You say tom*ah*to, I say tom*ay*to. And you say arse, and I say ass."

Fifteen

Robert joined up with Pacho in Florencia, where they booked into a hotel with a dirty swimming pool and a sign in the lobby warning clients not to take under-age girls into their rooms. It wasn't a very safe town, so Robert and Pacho stayed inside and drank beer and a small bottle of rum and then some *aguardiente* to pass the time. Later, they ordered a filling and unsatisfying meal which arrived in plastic bags from a Chinese restaurant and went to bed early.

Geri picked them up at six in the morning for the drive to San Vicente and they completed the trip without incident and went for lunch at the Toro Negro where they found Pardo, who was waiting for them with a freelance cameraman. Pardo had perked up considerably since Robert had last seen him. His face was red from the heat but he was smiling and drinking a steady stream of beers. His cough had gone.

"Order a good lunch. It might be our last decent meal for a few days," he said. He was wearing a baseball cap and a rather clichéd photographer's jacket with multiple pockets.

They ordered steak with rice, salad and chips, with beer. The beer cleared Robert's head from the night before.

"This time I really hope there's no booze where we're going. I need a break," he said to Pacho.

"Need a break from what? Beer is food, not alcohol," said Pardo, "It doesn't do you any harm. That's all exaggeration to scare the masses."

He lit a cigarette.

Pacho didn't usually talk much about stories he was working on, but, during the previous night in Florencia and the drive to San Vicente, he had become quite nervous about the trip with Pardo. Now he brought up the subject again.

"This story isn't going to make us very popular is it? Not with the government or the army," he said.

"Maybe not," said Pardo, "But there's nothing we can do about that, is there?"

Robert could see that Pardo and Pacho would make a good team. They would take turns scaring each other.

The story was this: the rebels were going to release a group of soldiers they had been holding prisoner, but first they wanted to show pictures of them still in captivity. Alfredo didn't trust most of the Colombian media, so he had asked Pardo to find a foreign journalist and he had proposed Robert.

After lunch, they packed their gear into the back of a pick-up truck, whose driver had, on Pardo's instructions, parked it in the sun outside the Toro Negro. A FARC guerrilla was leaning against a wall and watched them as they loaded the car, but he frowned and looked at the ground when Robert spoke to him. He was a small man, in his early twenties perhaps, and had a dark face and high cheek-bones. He was quite photogenic and Pacho took a picture of him, but then he turned round and faced the wall like a boy being punished in an old fashioned school.

Robert climbed in and sat crammed between Pardo and Pacho and they drove out of San Vicente, following a dirt track into the hills. Pardo closed the window because of the dust, but opened it soon afterwards because the heat became unbearable and then closed it again. After about an hour, he offered round a flask of whisky. Robert took a drink but felt sick in his stomach from booze and lack of air and the vibration of the car and shook his head when Pardo passed the flask around a second time.

Just before dusk they got to a town where there was nowhere for them to stay. The sun sank behind a black ridge of trees and the dirt road and the single row of roughly-built wooden houses turned briefly blue-silver before going grey. Dim lights began to glow in each of the shacks, and Pardo went from house to house looking for somewhere for them to spend the night, until finally he came back and told them to bring their sleeping bags. He had found two rooms in a farmhouse, and Robert and Pacho took possession of one and Pardo and his camera-man of the other. The woman of the house brought them rice and beans and grainy coffee, and they ate in the glow of a gas lamp before going to their beds. There was no elec-tricity in the village, but the woman played music loud on a battery-operated radio until late at night. Robert had spread his sleeping bag on a rubber mat placed on the dirt floor, but his head ached and he lay awake for hours scratching at insect bites. A cockerel crowed regularly throughout the night, and they could hear a pig some-where nearby. Pardo's cameraman already had diarrhea on his first day out of Bogota, and Robert heard him get up several times to go to an outhouse and afterwards wash his hands in a barrel of rainwater.

The next day they would meet Alfredo.

One of the soldiers, when the journalists pushed back the palm frond barriers and entered the camp, had been lying on his side watching a praying mantis stalk a fly.

"It moved so fast," he said, and his eyes wandered as he searched for words, "It looked like it just shivered. But then it had the fly."

He didn't know what to say.

"There's nothing," he said, "so selfish as a praying mantis."

A group of twenty had gathered round them in the mud like the lost boys, cheering at first and clamping them with slimy handshakes, then quiet and confused.

They had got religion and then lost it.

It seemed that the more you looked into yourself under the dark green canopy, the less you saw. Just the mud world, the stick world, the leaf world, where walking always took you back to the same place and smells were everywhere like light. Where patience meant as little as haste.

"They've strayed," said one of them, with a sad, superior smile. He alone had kept the faith.

Their faces were white or yellow or tinted green. They hadn't seen the sun properly for years, just felt its glimmer second-hand, rationed through the trees.

When they had fallen sick, the guerrillas had tried to help in their way. With aspirin. Aspirin for malaria, and for the fever and dysentery which came with it, when they passed blood in their stools and hallucinated. Each of them had gone through that several times. And aspirin too for leishmaniasis, which ate into their flesh and which they tried to burn away with matches.

The guerrillas, being peasants, were like herdsmen – not consciously cruel, but aloof – and tended to their prisoners as if they were cattle.

The camp was built within a stockade of wood, sharp palm fronds and barbed wire lain around a circle of trodden earth, where the soldiers had constructed their own bivouacs, lean-tos covered by camouflaged tarpaulins and raised on wooden platforms. There was no break in the tree canopy above them, and they lived in a green submarine light, floating on a raft of mud through a mist of mosquitoes, breathing a still air of mud and leaves, the scents of their own insect-bitten bodies blending with the mud.

"English? Which football team do you support?"

Several of them were shouting at the same time. Others stood by and giggled.

Robert didn't actually support any football team but said, "Manchester United."

"*El Manchester! Qué bueno!*" They all cheered. They jumped up and down. Some of them still wore fragments of army uniform. Others wore shorts and t-shirts. They all stank.

Pardo said to Robert, "They were boys when they were caught, seventeen, eighteen years old. So they've come of age here."

One said, "Do the people still remember us?" and the others went quiet.

"They don't remember us. We've been forgotten."

"Forgotten."

Pardo was mobbed as he shared out cigarettes, and his cameraman filmed him. Pacho was moving around trying different angles, snapping all the time. Robert was using his notebook and cassette recorder.

When the soldiers thought the guerrillas couldn't hear them, they asked if it was really true that they were going to be released.

"They told us they are going to let us go, but we don't believe them. We don't trust them. Are they telling the truth?"

"I think so," said Robert. "That's why they've brought us here."

"Can it really be true?"

"Just imagine if it is."

"I think it is," said Robert. "They're going to move you

172

to a place where they're going to hand you over to the government."

"And there's something else we're worried about," said one of the soldiers. "They've taken away our officers. What have they done with them? Are they going to let them go too?"

"I don't know about them," Robert said. It was a lie, but an easy one.

He turned on his tape recorder and asked one of them about how they'd found God. One night, in the camp, Jesus had begun talking to one of the prisoners, and he'd told the others and some of them had heard Jesus too. They had made up their own hymns and sung them, and prayed together and, for a few minutes at a time, it hadn't mattered so much where they were or what they might never see again.

"But they didn't have the strength," said the soldier, who kept apart from the others now. He had been the first to hear Jesus and was now the only one who had kept the faith. "It's difficult here, I understand. But they didn't have the strength to listen to the Lord."

The soldiers had a radio and one of them kept a journal in a child's exercise book, with a picture of Mickey Mouse on the cover. The best times for them were at night, when they listened to a radio program in which relatives of people who had been kidnapped could send messages. Several times, during their three years in captivity, one of the soldiers had heard his mother's voice, or a girlfriend's, although that had happened less frequently as time passed.

Eventually, when it was time to go, one of them said to Robert, as if trying to excuse himself, "We fought a whole day before we surrendered."

"Don't forget us," they said.

"I won't," said Robert, and Pardo smiled and grinned like everybody's uncle. Pacho and the cameraman shook hands with everyone.

Alfredo swaggered up through the sucking mud and made a speech for the camera, hooking his thumbs into his pockets and leaning backwards so his belly reared hugely beneath his camouflaged jacket. He wore a pistol in a holster. The soldiers looked away, but listened as he spoke. Their faces were sad and beaten. He addressed them as "boys", and it seemed an appropriate term. Alfredo continued for some time, smiling with pleasure beneath his moustache and modulating his voice for rhetorical emphasis. It was strange to hear him go on for so long without swearing, but he was speaking like a politician, like a man, Robert thought, who didn't expect to spend his whole life hiding in the jungle.

"Well, boys, I am happy to inform you that your long ordeal, an ordeal which wasn't our fault or even your fault, but was forced upon us all by the circumstances of a just war against an unjust society, that that ordeal is almost over. You will be free to return to your families, to your friends and loved ones. I know it has been hard for you, exposed to the wind and rain, to the heat and the cold, but of course these are the hardships which we revolutionary fighters suffer every day. The difference is that we chose this path willingly in order to fight against tyranny, but in your case it was forced upon you. Now, you might very well resent the loss of years of your youth, locked up in a camp. That would be natural. But when, in the comfort of your own homes, you think back on your time with us, I trust that any bitterness or resentment will be turned against those who are truly responsible, the oligarchs and class criminals who sent you working-class boys to fight against your own kind in the first place and then abandoned you once you were taken into custody by the FARC, the legitimate people's army."

After he had finished speaking, Alfredo led the journalists away as the prisoners looked on from inside their pen. The soldiers had watched the fat rebel commander with fear and hatred and Robert felt as if he had already betrayed them by strolling off with their captor to continue the propaganda tour.

"Those sons of bitches," said Alfredo, in his peasant accent. "They can be a cheeky lot. We have to be tough. Fair but *hijueputa* tough."

"How's that, *comandante*?" enquired Pardo.

A guerrilla brought them mess tins of river water coffee, and Alfredo checked that his had come without sugar. They were sitting on wooden benches surrounded by olive green bivouacs. They had only walked fifty metres from where the prisoners were held, but already it was silent, except for the jungle sounds of dripping leaves, wood cracking under foot.

"They fight, the bastards. We have to break fights up,"

175

said Alfredo, and he said it with a smile, with that strange, misplaced affection he seemed to have for everyone who really should hate him, an affection which against all reason expected to be reciprocated.

"What about escape?" asked Robert.

Alfredo spat, and looked at him for slightly too long.

"Escape? *Hijueputa!*" he said.

Pardo was silent.

"Surely some of them must have tried to escape, even if it was only once?"

"Yes," said Alfredo, eventually, "Once. One of them sweet-talked one of our girls and they both ran off. We've had all-male guard duty since then. Can't trust the silly bitches."

"Did they get away? Did they make it?" asked Robert.

This was apparently in poor taste. But, before Alfredo had time to consider a response, Pardo said, "Even if they did escape, it must be impossible for them, no, *comandante*? How could they find their way out of this jungle? How could they eat? What the hell would they do if they escaped? They're better off where they are."

Alfredo chuckled. Oh yes, a happy thought, all right.

"One day they'll understand. One day, once we've achieved what we're fighting for, they'll thank me," he said. "Because it's boys like that who are the people we're fighting for, working-class boys who've never had a chance in life. You never see any of those rich bastards in the army, they send our own kind to fight against us."

He spoke with the cheerful conviction of a happy psychopath, the unmalicious cruelty of a bully so complete that he interpreted any attempt at rebellion on the part of those he tormented as self-harm. He beamed, ruddy-cheeked, beneath his beret. Robert, to his own disgust, occasionally found himself liking Alfredo. Did the prisoners feel the same? What would they do with him if, by some miracle, they could render him defenceless? Would they end up asking forgiveness?

That afternoon they passed back into the clutches of Hugo, Alfredo's unbalanced sidekick. He didn't look pleased to see Robert and Pacho again. Robert, as previously, took pleasure in offending him. It was so easy, he deserved it so much, and his means of retribution were so few. Then Hugo, who had the task of driving them out of the jungle to a camp inside the demilitarised zone, hit upon the petty torture of refusing to stop for his passengers to urinate. As usual, there was a macho guerrilla subtext to this behaviour, which, to his muddled mind, demonstrated the inferiority of their bourgeois bladders. Even Pardo, who sat hunched in the front seat smoking cigarettes and swigging from a six-pack of Poker beer, disliked Hugo.

"Why are you such a bitter son of a bitch?" he asked, as Robert squirmed on the back seat of the stolen pick-up truck, the pressure already unbearable after just two Pokers.

"I'm not bitter. I just don't want to waste any time just because they're *maricones*, just because they're faggots."

But Hugo smiled as he spoke. He resented Pardo too,

but was scared of him. He flexed his long-nailed fingers on the steering wheel, moving them suddenly like the wings of a beetle.

"*Maricón serás vos,*" said Pacho.

"You can't say that," said Hugo.

"I just did. You're the faggot."

Hugo had stowed his AK47 in the back seat, where it was wedged between Robert and Pardo's cameraman, who held his big camera on his knees the whole time without complaining. Two empty beer cans were rattling by Robert's feet. The others, including Hugo, had just thrown theirs out of the window into the jungle.

"I'm a guerrilla," said Hugo.

He was hoping they would say something that wasn't just against him personally but was against the FARC.

"You're a fairy," said Pacho.

Finally, Hugo stopped the car. They had been driving along a road cut by the guerrillas through the jungle and paved with wooden planks on top of the mud. Pardo and Robert stood and urinated into the bushes.

"You know," said Pardo, as he pissed, "This is the life. I couldn't imagine living any other way."

Robert knew what he meant.

"Nor could I," he said.

"I've sacrificed everything for this. You know, I've got a little girl too," said Pardo, and then he concluded by saying, "I'll tell you later."

Hugo started the pick-up truck and began to move off

without them, forcing them to jog along the road of planks to catch up, pulling up their flies as they ran. They drove through the jungle for about an hour more, rolling forward slowly to keep traction on the slippery mud, sliding off the planks and then regaining them as Hugo steered wildly. The jungle looked dark and lifeless, and, in the moments when they were forced to stop, the only detectable movements were those of the seepage of water from the covering of leaves down to the muddy undergrowth and the mazy swirl of gnats and mosquitoes. Then they left the jungle and drove out onto open savannah along a dryer road of stones and deep red mud. Soon, the sun set, and it looked like there was a brushfire a few miles away across the golden-green grass.

Hugo put the radio on and found a signal, the typical discordant but rhythmic accordion and wail, which superimposed itself over the pick-up truck's vibration as it bumped and heaved over the road in the dark. Robert's head was bouncing against the metal window frame, but he was too tired now even to want the trip to end. His thoughts shimmied dreamily around the borders of discomfort, leaving no memories behind as he slipped in and out of sleep. At first he thought about the soldiers, locked in their pen in the jungle, feeling their way beneath mosquito nets to blankets folded above a padding of leaves. And he thought he'd like to do something for them, but what? He'd write an article, that's all, that's where his goodwill was going to go. The window frame was rattling against his head, and he opened his eyes in the darkness. Then, when he closed them again, he remembered his daughter, when she was very small, climbing up onto some tree stumps in a park and jumping off, then climbing back up again. The sun shone on her blond hair, and she was wearing a denim dress. Her face had a look of concentration when she climbed, and when she jumped she would shout. The stumps had been cut and left in a group for children to climb on, scattered like giant knucklebones on the grass, and the little girl had run up to them straight away. Robert just stood by in the sunshine, happy, not quite bored, watching her play, and taking her sticky hand when she held it out to stop herself from falling. She climbed and jumped, and climbed and jumped, again and again and again.

Why had he left her behind? He couldn't really remember. It just hadn't worked out with her mother. But why, exactly? He couldn't really say. That was too complicated. People said so many things to each other it was impossible to remember them all, or make sense of them all. And it was so hard to work out what you really wanted for yourself, anyway, so how could you possibly tell what other people wanted? It just hadn't worked out, and that was a shame. But his daughter still bobbed regularly into his mind, her hair shining in the sun, her fingers sticky, growing up somewhere. It hadn't worked out, and the point, Robert now knew with sad clarity, as his head thumped against the metal window frame, was not to analyse why. That was a cop-out, that wasn't it at all.

He felt very small again that night, in the cramped car crossing the savannah beneath the stars. He felt small within his own mind, channel-hopping between intense but unrelated memories. His little blond daughter, playing somewhere far away, maybe thinking of him sometimes. The man whose brains had been shot out as he leant back in a chair in a drug-trafficking town. Jesse, that boy who called himself Martín. And Milena. Milena, his beauty. That wasn't working out either.

His memories were like his journalism: fragments of meaning, unredeemed by responsibility. Memories like islands. Memories like theme parks, which you enter but have to leave when your time is up. Memories which will die.

Sixteen

Pardo had a way of tightening his cheeks when he exhaled smoke from a cigarette, as if he was about to smile. But he didn't. He looked like someone had hit him.

"Bad dreams," he said, "I don't always sleep so well."

The dawn light still hadn't warmed up. They were sitting on a log which seemed wet through their jeans but was mainly just cold. The jungle was leaking and crackling. Pardo blew out more smoke and looked on the verge of being happy again. The bags under his eyes had expanded and his whole face had puffed up, so his features flattened out.

"Not even here. I can't even sleep here," he said.

"What is it?"

"Fear," he said. "It's fear"

"Of what?"

"I don't know. It's just fear," said Pardo.

His voice was hoarse, too.

"It's tough spending the night in one of those bivouacs. I didn't sleep well myself," said Robert.

This time Pardo did smile, and Robert almost flinched.

"So," he said, "you're going to go to see the gringo?"

Robert didn't want to do it like this. But he just didn't trust Pardo.

"Alfredo's given permission," he said.

"For you?"

"For us, for me and for Pacho."

"You know you're only here because I invited you, because of my contacts?"

"I know."

"And Alfredo's not here. We just left Alfredo. You didn't say anything."

"I'm sorry."

"Well fuck you, mister," said Pardo.

He coughed.

"Fuck you," he said again when he had finished.

"It's just the way things worked out," said Robert.

And that was true, he thought, events had a way of separating him from people like that. It was the lack of a certain type of energy.

"Sure," said Pardo.

Sunshine fell through the trees. It was getting to be properly daytime. The guerrillas were moving slowly around doing chores. Two of them dug a latrine pit, halting regularly and gossiping in whispers. A girl, her long ponytail swinging beneath her beret, used her hands to pack leaves around sticks to light a fire. Robert saw Hugo preening himself by a lean-to, keeping a thumb beneath his rifle strap as he pushed his other hand through his heavy, damp hair. The camp had a dull, institutional feel. Combat seemed far away, an excuse for something rather than a purpose. No one appeared to be inspired by the hope of ultimate victory or at all concerned by the possibility of defeat. No one dreamed of anywhere else. Guns were everywhere, but even violence was just another routine, something for which the organisation took responsibility, demanding a necessary, boring cruelty.

"I'm sorry," he said to Pardo, but left it at that.

Pardo looked old and beaten-up. He sat hunched over on the log, smoking and nodding his white-haired head. Pacho asked what was wrong and Robert told him. The photographer took this two ways. Firstly, he went over to Pardo and patted him on the back, and, while Robert couldn't hear what he was saying, he was pretty sure he was disassociating himself from such ungenerous behaviour. But Robert knew he didn't really care about bilking Pardo. It was just competition. Pacho packed quickly, said goodbye to Pardo and his cameraman, from whom he bummed a few cigarettes, and hiked over to where Robert was waiting by the truck with the smarmy, insecure Hugo.

Pacho had worked out a strategy of asking Hugo slightly offensive favours very quickly.

"Mind taking this? It's difficult with my cameras."

He passed him his heavy backpack and got into the pick-up, laughing.

Hugo had been persuaded to drive them to San Vicente, where Robert intended to get a taxi for Martín's camp. Robert didn't want to go all the way with Hugo, so he pretended that he had to buy some audio cassettes in San

Vicente and said they could take a taxi for the rest of the journey. They had permission from Alfredo, so the taxi driver would have no trouble getting there. It was all within the odd, cultish safety of the demilitarised zone.

They drove along the dirt road through low hills, gulping dust. Occasionally they passed small wooden houses, the children bare-footed, their parents bewildered, gaping, prematurely gnarled. It was pretty country, unintensively farmed, with woods and copses, twinkling streams and green fields, like a heated-up England. But it wasn't. Robert shifted his arm from the window frame, where it was turning radish-pink in the sun. The tropics are corrosive, he thought, it's all sweat and stings and poison.

"This time he'll go on camera?" asked Pacho, shouting over the crash and rattle. He asked the question even though he already knew the answer.

"That's what he says," yelled Robert.

"Great story," said Pacho.

Hugo pointed a long-nailed wood sprite's finger at a billboard near San Vicente which called for recruits to the FARC. Rebels were painted as gleeful, life-sized blobs of primary colours, packing AKs. It wasn't so much socialist realism as socialist infantilism.

"Good, eh?" said Hugo. "We're the bosses around here. Not the government, not the Yankees."

"Very good," said Robert.

"Painting signs about the FARC doesn't feed anyone, does it?" said Pacho.

"What?" said Hugo.

But Pacho just shook his head.

They halted at a single-lane bridge behind an old Ford pick-up loaded with smiling peasants and a sole, disconsolate pig. A truck trundled in their direction, belching smoke and soot, its wheels wobbling as if about to fall off. The pig did not want to cross the bridge, making the peasants laugh. Robert repeated to himself what he had been thinking all morning, that he was going to tell Martín he couldn't help him. Hugo said he was hungry.

They entered San Vicente. The noisy, impoverished boom town was strung with paper decorations, and phony everything was on sale. It was a town where nothing was free but everything was cheap. They pulled up in a dirty square, near a queue of perspiring taxi drivers, and Robert bought the idiot Hugo a fizzy malt drink and an empanada.

"Maybe we could go and say hello to Yasmín," said Pacho.

"I've had enough of small town girls," said Robert.

"A man can never have enough of small town girls. You just have to play the field and keep your budget under control."

"I haven't done either."

Pacho laughed, but it was commiseration. He drank some of his Pony Malta. Hugo had already driven away, too conceited to be suspicious.

Robert ate though he wasn't hungry, looking around at the townsfolk with distaste. He looked at the skinny guys in singlets and the sweaty fat guys and the girls in cheap lycra, popping their cleavages. You've all cut your deals, haven't you, he thought. And he looked at the kids, at the little girls in pretty, cheap dresses, and the boys with their hair greased into parts, and he thought, you're going to learn pretty soon how to live with killers and sell yourselves. Love here meant spoiling and a lesson in selfishness. And the old people, too, bent and sagging, smelly and decrepit. Sold, sold long ago.

There were loudspeakers playing music on posts around the square. Robert felt he would like to smash them.

"Let's get a taxi then," he said.

Most of the taxis were the same: beaten-up yellow sedans. None of them would have any extra room in the boot. The driver they chose was fat, and he had a red pick-up truck instead of the usual cab. Better for the rough roads but very open.

"Last time I was here, the guy who drove us was called Víctor. Skinny guy. Know what happened to him?" asked Robert from a back seat, as they drove out of town.

The driver nodded.

"Yes, I know what happened," he said. "We all face that. We have to live with that. But I've got kids, I've got to work."

"Who did it?"

The guy shrugged his lardy shoulders, which barely permitted him to fit into the driver's seat. He raised his hands from the steering wheel in a brief but reckless gesture of ignorance.

"Only God knows."

"And whoever did it," said Robert.

"He talked too much," said the driver, and left it at that. Clearly he did not intend to commit the same mistake.

Robert sighed, and realised he had been sighing all morning. He was going to say no to Martín, he thought, and blew out his breath in a shudder.

"Fuck," he said, in English.

His thoughts were humming along now, trivial but compulsive. He was buzzing through an abstract picture gallery in his head.

This is pretty real, he thought, oh yeah. Adrenaline makes you a whole person. It reminds you your body's in charge. This is a very unsuburban experience, pure in its way. This is what journalism's all about. And then, my daughter, he thought, and then, Milena.

They were back among the pretty hills and fields. But there were buzzards, like the bad breath of landscape, and deformed, Quasimodo cattle, with giant bat ears and swinging pouches of surplus skin. After about two hours, they cleared the crest of a hill and a couple of rebels ran out onto the road from among some eucalyptus and waved for them to stop. Others would be covering them from the trees. They made them get out of the truck and asked for identity papers.

"*Buenos días*. Journalists. *Periodistas*," said Robert.

The driver leant against his car and smiled as one of the guerrillas puzzled over Robert's cedula.

"Oh, you want mine too?" said the driver. "Of course."

He fumbled with stubby fingers in a black velcro wallet full of saint's cards.

"Gringo," said the guerrilla looking at Robert's document.

He said it in a pensive way, wondering whether he should be aggressive or not, as if pronouncing the hateful word would help him to an answer, by allowing him to feel its sound. He was looking at Robert but avoiding his eyes. He was short and scrawny and about twenty years old, with a fuzz of moustache above his dark upper lip.

"No, not gringo. *Inglés*," said Robert. And then he said, "We've got an appointment with Martín. It's been approved by Alfredo."

At first it was as if they hadn't heard him, so he said it again. One of them hitched his Kalashnikov strap higher on his shoulder and mumbled that they would have to check at the camp. For once the delay was welcome to Robert. The bureaucratic predictability of FARC procedure calmed his nerves. It was cool on the road in the shade of the eucalyptus. Pacho gave the second guerrilla a cigarette, which attracted his comrades, who had been covering them from the trees. They strolled over and giggled. A strong breeze rushed through the leaves. Eventually, the first guerrilla came back and said they could continue, and they got into the truck and turned off the main road down a track through the wood. The site was so accessible and yet so exotic that it reminded Robert of a drive to a wildlife park for a fake safari. The camp was one of the semi-permanent sites the guerrillas had built in the demilitarised zone during the peace talks with the government. A dozen simple structures made of logs and plywood stood on sand cleared of vegetation by the acid of eucalyptus leaves. Most of them were just frames without walls: roofs covering spaces for wood stoves or benches or hard timber bunks. But Robert also saw a parabolic antenna for satellite TV and some of the better huts had doors and private rooms.

They got out of the car and asked the driver to wait until they were finished. A group of rebels watched them silently, with their rifles at the ready, as they sat down on a bench.

They said *buenos días*, and one or two mouthed inaudible replies.

"We're here to see Martín," said Robert, but it didn't seem to register. "Just wanted to make sure they knew," he said to Pacho.

"He'll come. Let's just stay here. They know who we are."

The day had turned overcast but it was very warm and the light was still harsh, making Robert squint. He was wearing a baseball cap to protect his face but his forearms were red and sore. He felt tired from the heat, and from four hours on the road. He looked around at the camp and now he wanted to get it over with. Now the prospect of waiting there any time at all seemed intolerable.

"It must be pretty damn boring living here, don't you think?" he said in a low voice.

He had crossed his legs and was jigging one foot up and down.

"Boring isn't the word," said Pacho.

"And these guys can't even go to the toilet to take a shit without permission."

"That's the same as in the army."

"No, the army gives you time off, and then eventually you serve your time and they let you go. These guys don't let you go ever."

"They're fighting for the cause."

"They're fucking out of their minds."

Pacho laughed.

It was still wasn't midday, but felt later. A day or longer could pass until the guerrillas found Martín and he responded to their message. Time on its own barely seemed to matter to these people. What was important to them was the combination of time and distance. The time it took to cross a hill covered in jungle. The time it took to travel by river from one camp to another. One of the rebels once told Robert he reckoned distance in terms of how far he could walk before needing another cigarette. There were five-cigarette journeys, ten-cigarette journeys. Twenty cigarettes was a very long way.

Half an hour passed. An hour.

Just to say something, Robert said, "What's the most boring thing you've ever had to do?"

"I'm always bored," said Pacho. "I think that's why I became a photographer, because I didn't want to get bored."

"But you're bored now. Just look at us."

"But I don't mind it here, out in the country. It's in the

town that I get bored. Although I prefer being in town."

"You prefer being bored?"

"No, I like girls and beer, and driving around. I like television a lot. A real lot."

"The problem is that people can't concentrate these days. We can't sit down and read a book or work on a problem without getting fidgety. You know I think television's got something to do with that. All that television we watched when we were kids."

"Uhuh," said Pacho.

"I'm bored now. I'm kind of worried and bored at the same time. It's weird. It's like a boring nightmare. It seems impossible, but it isn't."

A mosquito bit Robert on the arm. He slapped at it, but it was too late. Then he heard something, looked up and there was Martín. It was a surprise to see again how much of a kid he was, a kid with a beard which just looked like dirt.

He was very nervous. He was grinning and held out his hand, but glanced to one side and then back again.

"Well, well, well," he said. "Well, well. Here you are. *Aquí estamos.*"

"Hello, Martín," said Robert.

And, to his surprise, he felt the guy was a friend. Martín looked at him with his crazy, darting brown eyes, and kept on grinning, somehow. He was accompanied by a man of about forty who carried a pistol instead of a rifle, whom he introduced as Juan Antonio Márquez, the camp commander. Márquez said, "What are the rules?"

He meant the rules to determine what people would see on television.

"Rules?" said Martín, and Robert replied, "It's an interview, that's what we agreed with Alfredo. On camera. We'll set it up and have a chat. I'm sure Alfredo's told you."

"Are you going to speak in Spanish, or in your other language?"

Márquez was kind of stylish for a guerrilla. He had long black hair, worn under a slouch hat, a moustache like twin glistening tassels, and a compact, neatly defined figure. All in all he had a sort of rebel dash. But he was short, and there wasn't anything he could do about that. He wasn't smiling.

"In English, it has to be in English," said Robert.

"There's no problem is there? No problem with that?" asked Martín.

"I prefer Spanish. So we can all understand," said Márquez.

Jailbait, thought Robert, but hairy.

"No," he said, "It has to be in English. That's the deal. Alfredo knows that."

Robert felt very comfortable with this type of professional argument, as if he was a lawyer or an official spokesman. It relaxed him.

"But how do I know what he's saying is correct?"

"Alfredo said we could do it that way."

"He did, yes," said Martín.

Pacho asked where they could do the interview.

"I still haven't decided whether it's going to happen yet," said Márquez.

"Isn't that Alfredo's decision?" said Robert. It was his only argument but it was a good one. So he shut up and waited for it to take effect. Márquez looked like his head hurt.

"I want to listen to every word," he said finally.

"That's fine by me. You're welcome to," said Robert.

Pacho unfolded a tripod for the video camera and asked if Márquez could lend them a couple of chairs.

"He doesn't look very happy," said Robert to Martín, as the commander went off in search of the props.

"He hates me. Because I'm a gringo. So he thinks that I think that I'm better than he is."

"How are you getting on?"

Martín lost his grin. He was very pale.

"I'm here. Just look around you. How do you think I am?"

"Yeah."

"I'm stuck."

"You know," said Robert, "I don't think we can help you out. Sorry."

It was what he had to say and it couldn't wait.

The young American looked at his rubber boots.

"I kind of figured," he said, and Robert could see him swallow. "But maybe there is something you can do for me. Just a little thing."

Márquez returned before he could finish what he wanted to say, followed by a rebel carrying two plastic garden chairs, one in each arm.

Robert took a swig from a bottle of mineral water he had bought in San Vicente. He took off his baseball cap, wiped his forehead with his hand and passed a comb through his hair. He had written down some questions for the interview in his notebook and tried to put them in order in his mind. It was best to concentrate on the interview now he had disposed of that other business. But he felt shaky.

"Do I look too red?" he asked.

"You look okay. Just pat your hair down a bit more on top," said Pacho.

Pacho positioned the chairs in the dirt by a tree and told Martín to sit down so he could look at the image through the viewfinder. Martín laid his rifle against the tree, but Pacho asked him if he could sit with it on his lap.

"Perfect. That's the way. You look like a real guerrilla now," said Pacho, hunched over the small camera, which was balanced on the tripod.

Martín was smiling, sitting there with his gun, but Robert couldn't tell whether the expression was genuine.

"I am a real guerrilla," said Martín. He was speaking his American Spanish.

"We are all guerrillas," said Márquez, glowering in the shade.

"Sure, but no one will know about it unless we film you properly," said Pacho, positioning a chair for Robert just to one side of the camera, so that interviewer and lens shared almost the same line of vision. It was Pacho who was in control now. Not Márquez in his own camp, not even Robert, but the cameraman he had hired. Pacho slipped a small microphone through one of Martín's button holes.

"Could you say something please? Just say anything you like."

"Long live the people's revolution," said Martín, grinning.

A bird, perched somewhere in the eucalyptus wood above the sandy camp, began to squawk.

"Say something else please, just keep on talking."

"Oh, I don't know. We had sancocho for lunch."

"Great. That's perfect. Could you sit down as well now, Robert?"

Pacho hooked Robert up to another mike and did a sound check.

"Just start talking please."

Robert asked his first question, which he had written down. It was conceived for television, a mini pre-judgemental narrative all in itself. Robert heard his voice change as he read it out, becoming bold and blankly confident, a resonant if perhaps oddly uninquisitive voice for questions, a television voice.

"Why did a young American, a college student with a good future, join a rebel army in Colombia?"

Frowning, trembling slightly, straightening out his slouch, Martín began his story, speaking with a seriousness indistinguishable from sincerity.

"Well, here, I hoped my life would have meaning," he said. And then he mentioned selflessness. He spoke about how personal gain wasn't everything. War. Injustice.

"Stop please," said Pacho, "Okay, start again from the beginning now."

Martín was taken aback. His commander looked confused. Márquez was making a point of being seen to strain to hear the words, just so that they would never be quite sure that he didn't understand English.

Robert resonated again.

"Why did a young American, a college student with a good future, join a rebel army in Colombia?"

"Is this it now? Can I answer properly now?" said Martín.

"Yes, this is it. Go ahead."

"Why did a young American, a college student with a good future, join a rebel army in Colombia?"

"I hoped my life would have meaning here," said Martín. His voice broke slightly. He spoke again about his life at college. Then he mentioned the war in the 1950s, the way violence had been used against the democratic left. Very soon it was boring, not good TV at all, so Robert interrupted him with a second prepared question as he paused for breath.

"You wanted to be a hero?"

Martín smiled. He liked that word. "Yeah, what's wrong with that? That's a good thing, isn't it? Yeah, I wanted to be a hero."

Thank you very much, thought Robert, nice phrase, even if I did think of it myself. He didn't enjoy television work very much. It was too openly brutal, just too damn rude.

Martín kept on talking about Colombia. But television view-
ers weren't interested in Colombia; if they were interested at
all, they were going to be interested in Martín. They wanted
secrets and fears. If the story was going to sell, it was going
to have to appeal to voyeurs. In that sense it was literature.
The idea was to make Martín work as a character on TV for
10 minutes. One important question Robert wanted to ask
was "Would you kill an American?" Obviously, for the sake of
drama, Robert hoped the answer to that one was "Yes". The
other line of questioning was less generic, and based on
special knowledge of Martín's case. It was a betrayal of confidence. Robert remembered Klitsch's unpleasant but apt
phrase. He was a pornographer of pain. Many of the earlier
questions were decoys and Robert knew he could edit them
out later. He asked more about Marxism and Colombian
history and allowed Martín to drone on. It was unuseable
material. Martín talked about the UP and the gini index and
the bombing of the Casa Verde and didn't sound so
unhappy at all. He spoke with his special evangelical grin.
Robert nodded his head but his gaze wandered beyond
Martín's sloping shoulders to where a group of guerrillas
stood gaping at them. They would have been begging at traffic lights if they had lived at Bogota. They were enjoying the
scene, which was a confirmation of the importance of the
FARC. A breeze was blowing, and, together with the scent of
eucalyptus and the softening light, made the camp feel
fresh, dispelling its odour of sweat and latrine pits and
humid tropical mould and languor.

Here it comes.

"As a member of a rebel army, would you ever kill an American?"

Robert didn't enjoy asking that one. But the question wasn't so much his as dictated by the requirements of his profession. His voice became even firmer as he phrased it, its tones further removed from those of ordinary human communication, as if it were the utterance of some impersonal journalistic oracle, of the spirit of television itself.

Martín wasn't ready for it coming from Robert. But of course, it hadn't really come from Robert, it had come from Journalism. The young man's smile went away again and his eyes widened.

"Well, you get into situations. But, you know, I've never gotten into that one, into that particular situation."

He looked pretty ridiculous in his uniform now, with his gun across his lap.

"But if you were in that situation, as a rebel, if you did come across them in combat, say, you would kill them? Shoot at them with your rifle? With that rifle?"

"Hey, you know, I mean, I don't think it's fair for you to put me into a situation like that."

"But you are a rebel."

"I am a rebel, yes, a member of a guerrilla army."

"So you would shoot? Because that's what rebels do. Can we agree on that?"

"I would shoot."

"Even at an American?"

"Yes."

That was enough. The light of the oracle dimmed in Robert's bleary eyes. Martín would do what rebels do just as Robert did what reporters did. Or at least that's what Martín had said.

Then, into the newly sullen silence, toddled a quiet little question.

It began with the word Jesse, a sound that carried itself on tiptoes.

"Jesse, do you ever think you've made a mistake?"

Robert's voice had mellowed, his register softening from hollow provocation to unctuous empathy.

"Do you ever," he asked, solicitous now, really almost quite concerned, "worry that you're fighting someone else's war? Fighting someone else's war in someone else's country?"

Cliché is the journalist's friend. It's cute. It taps right into the vein, pilfering emotion. It's like a vampire bat in a Japanese cartoon.

"Mistake?"

Martín's voice was breaking again.

"I haven't made any mistake. No," he said, glancing at Márquez, who was frowning and had crossed his arms.

An early trace of a smile on his face, Martín looked at Robert and nodded. Come on, he was saying, come on. And Robert felt as if he was slipping away from something.

"Have you ever wanted to get away?" he asked.

That was it, or close enough to it. The words just came out. He had just been doing his job.

"No," said Martín, with a smile.

Robert, off camera, wiped the sweat from his face. Martín looked further away from him, smiling and distant. Robert asked a few more questions and Martín answered, questions about his family, about his life in the States and his life now, colour questions.

Once the interview was over, Pacho unhooked the small mike from Martín's shirt and repositioned the tripod so that the camera was pointing at Robert, who sat up straight and frowned.

Once again, he said, "Why did a young American, a college student with a good future, join a rebel army in Colombia?"

He said it even better and more resolutely than before. He was more relaxed now the interview had concluded. Then he sat still and nodded his head as if he was listening to the reply

"That's so phony," said Martín.

"I know. It's an old trick for when you've only got one camera. Half the stuff you see on TV's done like this. No one ever realises."

Robert helped Pacho fold up the tripod and gathered up his notebook and tape recorder. The American watched, holding his Kalashnikov.

"Hey, you shouldn't have asked that question, about wanting to leave," he said.

Robert put on his baseball cap. He wanted to get out of the camp as quickly as possible.

201

"I know, I'm sorry. You're right. But, you know it's a question which just had to be asked. Any journalist, even someone who knew nothing about you, would have asked it. And you answered it okay."

"I'm not even going to say what I think about it."

"Hey, I'm sorry."

And he smiled, a full, relaxed grin.

"You just don't give a shit, do you?"

"No, that's not true."

"Yes it is. But there isn't anything I can do about it, is there?"

"No," said Robert, "Look, I want to say thank you."

Martín laughed.

"You're welcome," he said.

Why was he laughing, thought Robert, and then, Oh well, good.

Up strutted Márquez.

It would have been fun to ask him whether he had enjoyed listening to the interview in English, but instead Robert said, "Thank you very much, comandante."

And then Martín asked Márquez a favour.

"If you don't mind, I'm just going to run into San Vicente with these journalists."

The commander waved his assent.

"You mean, you're coming with us?" asked Robert.

"Yes, just to San Vicente," said Martín. "I have to visit Nora. Don't worry, it's all within the zone."

Márquez was waiting for them to leave.

"Okay," said Robert, because he couldn't do anything to stop him.

They walked through the camp to where the driver was waiting with his truck. Pacho carried the tripod. Martín entered one of the huts and came out with a small ruck-sack.

"They let you go into San Vicente, then?" asked Robert.

"Oh yeah, anywhere within the zone, with the comman-der's permission. No problem. And I'm running an errand for Alfredo," said Martín. "It's a cage, but it's a big cage."

He was the first to get into the car, climbing into the back and placing his bag on his knees. The driver looked at him and then got in as well. You didn't bother the rebels with questions.

"He's coming with us?" asked Pacho.

"Just as far as San Vicente."

They got into the car. Robert hoped to make Florencia that night and to be in Bogota the next day. They had the tapes and the cameras with them on their laps and they had put the rest of their stuff in the back.

"Hey, I'm sorry for barging in on you like this," said Martín.

"No problem."

"It's just that I've got to run this errand, and I'd have had to have waited for another car. You know."

"Sure."

But it was a problem. Robert felt it was a problem.

The car started.

"You know," said Robert hoarsely, as they drove out of the FARC camp, watched by mute peasant fighters, "I feel sorry for you."

Pacho was sitting between them. They left the eucalyptus wood behind and drove out onto the main dirt road.

"Well, it's my own fault, isn't it?" said Martín, and he smiled again, opening his eyes very wide. He took off his beret and rubbed his curly hair. He had his AK pointing up between his legs.

"I've just got to live with it, man," he said.

"Yeah," said Robert.

He looked at his watch. It was about two o'clock. The clouds spread the rays of the sun all over the sky into a grey, universal glare which Robert registered more as weariness than as a quality of the light, something to do with his headache. The truck bashed and bumped like a failing jackhammer, straining dust through the few centimetres of open window. He wanted to ask Martín how he had ever put up with the Caguán. But he asked something else, leaning over Pacho and raising his voice.

"How's your mother?"

"My mother?"

"Yeah, she e-mailed me she was happy you'd contacted her."

"Shit man, I hate my mother," said Martín.

"Oh, okay," said Robert.

"She's a kook."

"Sorry?"

204

"A kook."

Robert felt better after this exchange.

"What are you going to do? You know, about your situation? What's the solution?" he asked.

"What am I going to do? Shit, the questions you ask."

"Sorry, I'm a journalist. It's a habit."

"It's still you who's asking those questions, and it's a bad habit."

They were driving back through the hills again, the hills so pretty that they weren't enough in themselves and made you think of somewhere else. But there was the swamp smell, the tang of sweat and insects, the rank odour of defeat.

Martín said, "Stop the car. I want to take a piss."

He got out with his rifle and his rucksack, which he slung over a shoulder as he positioned himself in front of a bush, legs splayed for comfort. Then, after bouncing up and down a few times and hitching his trousers, he took out a bottle of mineral water, swigging quickly before pouring the rest over his head, and a tube of cream which he began to rub over his beard.

"Hey, what's that?"

"Shaving cream," said Martín, smearing himself with his fingers.

He had put his rucksack on the ground next to his rifle.

"What the fuck are you doing with that?"

"I'm rubbing it into my beard, Robert. That's what it's for. Although it's not lathering up very well."

"You can't shave here."

205

Martín didn't reply. He took out a plastic disposable razor, and began to slash at his irregular growth.

"Jesus Christ, this hurts. It's like a fucking machete. Jesus Christ. I need a mirror."

"What the fuck are you shaving for, Martín?"

He picked up his rifle and the rucksack and manipulated one of the truck's side mirrors before crouching down on the side of the road.

"What's he doing?" asked the driver. "He can't do that."

"Stop it," said Robert.

"I think we should just go," said Pacho to Robert. He touched the driver on the shoulder.

"You can't do that, sir," said the driver and turned the key in the ignition.

"Hey, turn off the engine," said Martín.

The driver switched it off.

"It's best for everyone if I can do this quickly," said Martín, kneeling in the dirt. He was unclogging the razor by tapping it against the side of the truck.

"Why don't you film me, Robert?"

"No, I don't want to film this."

Robert and Pacho were sitting rigidly in the back seat.

"Go on. That's the whole idea, isn't it? Film me. You've got to get the whole story. You're supposed to be the journalists, Goddamn it. Film it, for fuck's sake."

"Why not?" said Pacho, and he took the video camera from its soft case.

Martín didn't look at all like Che Guevara any more. His

chubby face was raw and scratched. A few clumps of beard survived, like the first random sproutings of adolescence,

"I'm shaving my way to freedom," he said, speaking to the camera. "Look at this. Instant gringo."

The driver swivelled round, making an effort with his fat body and wedging his sweaty forearms on top of the seat, and asked Martín to let him go.

"Can't do that. He'd tip off the sentries, the pig," said Martín.

He moved back several paces from the truck, taking the gun with him, then pulled a pair of jeans and a t-shirt from his rucksack and wriggled and jumped out of his guerrilla uniform before putting them on.

Pacho was filming all the time from inside the car.

"I just wish I had some real fucking shoes. But I've only got these fucking boots," said Martín.

Then he lobbed his rifle into the bushes. "Don't worry, guys. I have a pistol," he said, taking it from his rucksack. "That rifle's just a bit cumbersome inside a truck."

He screwed his uniform into the bag and threw that away too, before climbing back into the truck next to Pacho and pointing the pistol at him. It wasn't anything personal, it was more that Pacho just happened to be in the next seat. Pacho focussed his camera and took a good shot of the pistol pointing at his belly.

"We're not going through San Vicente. We're going to go round the town straight onto the Florencia road," said Martín.

The driver turned the ignition key and they started.

"Go faster," said Martín. And then he said, "So, want to ask me any more questions?"

"Yes," said Robert. "What the fuck are you trying to do?"

"Don't swear so much, dude, or you won't be able to use this prime time."

"What are you playing at, Martín?"

And then he added "Jesse". He had remembered people would be watching in America and that Jesse was his real name, his American name.

The driver whimpered and groaned about his family, and Martín told him to keep quiet.

"Just remember, they're going to kill me if they catch me. For desertion," he said.

"Why don't you let one of us go? You don't need all of us," said Robert, "Why don't you let Pacho go, for instance?"

He couldn't help adding that "for instance". Just in case.

"Can't do that. Too risky. Hey, you're going to run out of batteries."

Pacho lowered the camera. His hands were shaking. He had been filming all the time, as if the lens were a magic charm which would protect him from what was on the other side.

"Jesse, you wouldn't really shoot us," said Robert.

"Yes I would. You've got to believe that, for your own safety. You've got to believe that. This is a rational decision. This is my fucking plan, man. It's logical."

Martín looked more euphoric, more excited and twitchy,

than resolute. He had pushed the pistol into Pacho's side, so that he could fire immediately anyone moved. Pacho, now that he had stopped the camera, was leaning back with his eyes closed. His swamp-like face had been drained of its usual uniform dun purple, leaving it mottled and blotched with small islands of irritation and solar haemorrhage.

Robert asked a question whose extreme irrelevance made it seem like a manifestation of courage.

"Have you got a girlfriend, Jesse? I mean in the FARC?"

Pacho opened his eyes and started filming again when Robert asked the question.

"Yeah, I've got a girlfriend. I neglected to say goodbye."

"It wouldn't have been wise. You had to get permission to see her?"

"Yep, from Márquez."

Then Robert said, "Ever kill anyone?"

"No."

"Were you disappointed by that?"

"At first, not any more though."

"Ever shoot at anyone and miss?"

"Nope."

"Not even that?"

"Nope. Hey, you should have asked that question in the interview. But you forgot, didn't you?"

"Why'd you change your mind about the FARC? Why do you want to escape?"

"It's not what I thought it was, Robert. They're not what I thought they were."

"You've done a pretty stupid thing, haven't you? You've screwed up."

"Yeah. I've screwed up. I admit that. I'm growing up, man. You've got to learn to admit to your mistakes when you grow up."

"Hey, Jesse, do you think we'll make it through the checkpoint?"

"I hope we do. I don't know if we will."

"What will they do to you if we don't?"

"I've already told you."

"Say it again on camera."

"They'll shoot me, Robert. They'll shoot me for desertion."

"You just wanted to be on television, didn't you? That's it, isn't it? That's the reason for all this FARC bullshit, isn't it?"

But Martín wasn't looking at Robert. He was holding the chunky black pistol into Pacho's ribs and watching the road ahead of them. Pacho was still filming.

"You're sick in the head," said Robert

"So are you, Robert."

"That's right," said Robert, "That's right. You're right there."

For most of the drive they were silent. It lasted for more than an hour, long enough for them to feel calmer, long enough for Robert to ask himself, repeatedly but in vain, whether everything wasn't all right after all. He noticed how Martín's expression changed without continuity from a grin to a frown, from determination to fear. Maybe he was looking for the right face for when the filming began again. His pistol hand would droop and then jerk back to the level of Pacho's guts. Robert could see he wanted to sleep. He was drowsy himself in the stifling air of the car.

They drove out of the unfarmed hills and into lower land, a flatter tarmac road leading through fenced-off cattle paddocks glowing green between the palm trees. A few drops of rain began to fall, sliding down the windscreen in dusty streaks, scouting the way for the coming cloud-burst. The sky was bluish grey.

Martín told the driver to stop.

"Get out and walk back to town," he said.

"My car," said the driver.

"You'll get it back. It's safer for you to get out."

"I can eat because of my car," said the fat man, but he got out anyway and stood in the rain. "My family has to eat," he said.

Martín told Pacho to drive. And then he said to Robert, "He's Colombian, it will look better. You'd better use the camera."

"You're nuts," said Robert.

"You guys aren't going to say anything," said Martín, "Because if you say something they'll kill me. And that'll be a story, won't it Robert? That'll be something which people will remember if they kill me because of you."

It was raining more heavily. Pacho got out and seemed to hesitate on the road before bowing his head and climb-ing into the front seat. He started the truck on the second attempt and they drove forward in silence for no more than a few minutes, crossing the ridge of a long, gradual hill. Then they saw the guerrillas at the checkpoint, hunched beneath the downpour.

The trick was to say as little as possible. They all knew that.

Robert climbed out of the truck and stood mute beneath the rain, waiting to be ordered to do something. He held up his arms for one of them to frisk him and then felt in his wallet for his identity card.

The rain turned everything grey. A flash of lightning made the rebels laugh. They had no waterproof clothing and the rain was filling their boots.

"Journalists. We were doing a story with Alfredo, and now we're going to Florencia. We were with Alfredo," said Robert, and got back into the car. Pacho got into the front.

Then came the problem with Martín, and Pacho started the engine. Robert just picked up the camera and filmed.

Seventeen

What business did that oval of water have, being black on a day like this? Blue-black, black-silver, but black, mirror-scuff black. Yet when the wind moved the pond's surface, it stirred a ripple of reflection, like the animated depiction of a tremor in space-time. Then he could see the sky in it: light blue, puffball clouds, rolling, shivering, but pulled inevitably back to centre.

Webbing prints muddied the concrete banks, like a scuffle at a crime scene. A breeze rushed through the trees, going somewhere. There was an aeroplane. There was always, eventually, in whatever corner of the sky he examined, a condensation trail, breaking up and losing its line.

It was the morning and so he had nowhere to go. The park was quite large, and he walked around it in large, slow circles. Then he lay down on the grass, and he felt like he was lying on an island in the sky. Outside the park was London. Nothing much happens in a park. That was the idea. It was a limbo place, where numb becomes calm. A place where consciousness laps on the border of itself. Thoughts came at him, but from a distance, foreign as the waterfowl.

He lay on his back and felt he was moving as he watched the clouds. He remembered what his little girl had said to him the day before and the memory made him laugh out loud.

"What," she had asked, in her cockney Jamaican accent, "are the five senses?"

"What are the five senses?"

"Yeah, what are they? Which ones?"

"Well, there's sight, looking with your eyes. Then there's hearing, touch, um, smell and taste."

This response caused mild disappointment.

"Oh. That's right," she said. Then, with obvious reluctance, she added, "Very good."

She hadn't remembered him at first, but she accepted him because he fitted into the category "father". She showed him to the neighbours. She had shown him more than introducing him. When he went to pick her up after school she showed him to her friends. "This is my Daddy," she had said, pointing.

At midday, he got up from the grass and walked across the park to a pub. Scraps of paper and ballooning crisp packets flittered around the pavement outside. Within there was a sort of lukewarm, oily temperature, comfortably lower than blood-level, spiced with smoke, and a continual ambient noise like a spade scraping a coffin. The smells were bitter yet warm, of cigarettes and beer, something not sweet but almost, it was more pleasantly astringent, the whiff of clean clothes and deodorant, of freshly-manufactured food wrapped in plastic.

Two men sat at an opposite booth. Slanting sunlight lit up their lagers, half-drunk and sudsy in pint glasses on the dark sticky table. Their close-cropped hair glowed like motes.

"And I said to him, well, you fucking sod you, well, you'd better fucking well fuck off you cunt or else I'll go and log a complaint I will, that's what I fucking said."

"Well fuck me dead."

"Fucking right. Yeah."

"Software business is like that these days."

"Guy fucks with your password-protected profile, he's fucking, fucking …. You've just got to say 'Oi!,' like, 'don't you do that'."

"Absolutely no respect for security procedures at all. None."

It was a profane yet rule-bound conversation, all violence confined to its aspirates. Later one of the men got up for another round and politely said "Thanks very much" to the woman behind the bar.

Robert had ordered a lasagne, which came with a token tuft of salad. When he finished, he pushed his plate away and a woman came and picked it up. He didn't want to leave yet, so he went to the bar and ordered another pint of bitter.

In an hour he could go to see his daughter. He visited her house every day like a boyfriend, dozing among the soft toys on her bed as she giggled and shouted at cartoons. But even the laziest, least attentive beau would have been compelled to heavier duties; what most mattered to her was his presence.

His presence was all he had right now. The status of foreign correspondent is unusual in that it is defined by exclusion, by being foreign. That didn't work any more. Not in Britain. Robert was at home and that meant he wasn't anything.

Something would turn up, he supposed. But people had other things on their minds at the moment. He had gone to see the foreign editor of a paper which had published his stories from Colombia, to see if he could help him out.

"Problem is, I can't go back," he had said.

"Yes, I see. Too dangerous."

"I'm even trying to sell my car from here. Not easy. But I had to get out in a hurry."

The foreign editor did a good job of appearing momentarily concerned. Robert had pulled up a chair in front of his desk in the newsroom.

"Well, maybe there's a positive aspect to it. The story isn't there any more. Not in Colombia. Not after what's just happened. It will be in the Muslim countries, the Middle East. That would be my long-term bet. So maybe in a few years, you'll look back and see that this change came at a good time for you."

"The story's in the Middle East, but I don't speak the languages. I think I need something in England," Robert had said.

"By the way, congratulations on that story. If you'd only got it out a week earlier, it would have been huge. But, the way things are, there just isn't the interest. We just didn't have the room for it. Sorry."

"No, of course," said Robert. He understood.

On his way back from the newspaper offices to the hotel in Earls Court where he was staying while he waited for his money to run out, Robert had stopped at an internet café to look at his e-mails. There had been several old ones from Martín, and he had deleted those. There was also a message from Luke, who was taking care of his remaining affairs in Colombia and wrote that Willie Wilcox had returned some of his CDs. An honest man, an honest bastard, thought Robert.

He had only spent two days back in Bogota, just long enough to buy a plane ticket for Gatwick. He had felt a strange, unjustifiable euphoria. There was an emotional mismatch, like the dizzy feeling after an illness, that feeling of hollow happiness, the sensation of being about to fall and not knowing whether to care. He had found his flat empty. Milena had taken her belongings and hadn't even left a note. He wouldn't have had any idea where she had gone if Wilcox hadn't rung on his first night, as he drank whisky after whisky in his underwear unable even to try to sleep.

Wilcox had spoken to him in an unnecessarily gruff way.

"She's left some stuff behind. A sort of blouse thing, I think. It's purple, or something," he said. "She wants it back."

217

"I didn't even know you knew her,"'said Robert.

He was in this odd, disoriented mood when he had arrived for an appointment at the U.S. embassy. He had still thought he had to finish the story about Jesse. The two officials who sat with him in a windowless room refused to let him use his camera.

"Dead?" said one.

"Killed? And he's an American?" said the other.

"Oh shit, what a screw-up."

"Where's he dead?"

"And why, why's he dead?"

"How?"

"But, you know, he deserved it all right," said the first one.

"Sure, he had it coming," continued the other. "So, tell us."

Robert, who meant to take a taxi straight to the airport when he left the embassy, explained what had happened and what he planned to do. But he couldn't show them the video right at that moment.

"You've got it on tape? And you're going to use it ..."

"For profit?"

"You bet," said Robert. "I risked my fucking life after all."

And maybe he did lack a moral compass. That was probably part of his problem. He'd just never had one, if anyone anywhere still did. He was lost in space.

"They call that a snuff movie, my friend," said the first official.

"I'm just a reporter. It's a story," said Robert.

He had it on video. He imagined it playing on a hundred million screens. Passing through the doors to hundreds of millions of minds.

He had been jet-lagged when he arrived in London. Time didn't seem right. People looked at him the wrong way. He went into a pub and the words just didn't come, so the girl behind the bar thought he had a stutter. He had travelled too quickly to too different a place. He had changed channels.

On the second afternoon, still feeling giddy, he had taken the underground train to the small house where his ex-wife lived. Angrily, she stood before him in the sitting room with her arms crossed. The place smelt artificial: of carpets and cleaning fluids. The television was on but she had turned down the volume.

"So, are you still a fake? Are you still pretending to be something you're not?" she asked.

"No," he said. "I don't know what to pretend these days. I've forgotten. Do you mind if I sit down?"

She looked at him sternly and went on with what she had been saying.

"Okay, if you're back then, we'll have to sort out access. There've got to be rules."

"Rules. Why? What rules?" said Robert.

And just as he said that, he was looking over her shoulder at an aeroplane crashing into a building in New York.

"Jesus Christ. Look at that. On the television," he said.

"Please will you just listen to what I'm saying?"

"But just look at that. Jesus Christ."

Standing in her small sitting room, his ex-wife refused to turn round. She was angry with him. The sky glowing on the screen had been a beautiful, searing, bright, bright blue.

It was only later, after an hour had passed and he had walked outside, that he realised his video didn't matter any more. That no one would care about that now. He could throw it away. And then he thought, poor Jesse, poor Martín or whoever he thought he was. He did have a moral compass but it was the wrong one. And he didn't get what he wanted, and nor will I.

His ex-wife stood there getting angrier.

"Listen to me Robert, will you. Whatever it is, it isn't as important as sorting this out," she said.

And then his daughter had come running down the stairs in a rush.